Annihilation

K. D. McAdams

This book is a work of fiction. Names, characters, places and incidents are figments
of the author's imagination or are used fictitiously. Any resemblance to actual
persons, living or dead, events, or locales is purely coincidental.

Cover design: Lacey O'Connor www.laceyoconnor.com

Interior design: K. D. McAdams

Version 1.26.14

Caveman Worldwide LLC

Copyright © 2013 K. D. McAdams

ISBN-13: 9780988958814

DEDICATION

For Jen, Lily, RJ and Justin.

I would drive anywhere with you.

- Dad

ACKNOWLEDGMENTS

A huge thank you to my family and friends who have read, shared and supported my work. Without a strong community my stories would still be floating in my head and leaving me to wonder.

CHAPTER 1

I am about to revolutionize the way the world generates and even thinks about power. Eight years of experimentation and self-taught physics have me days, possibly hours, away from achieving my dream—a dark energy reactor. I just need a little more time and some quiet to cull the final answers from the recesses of my brain where I know they must live.

I have spent half of my life on this invention. I have sacrificed almost everything that matters to most people my age. There have been no Homecoming dances, first kisses or game-winning goals. Experiments and research alone in my basement lair have consumed my sleeping and waking thoughts.

But I owe it to myself and, I think, to the world, to complete my work. While the goal started out selfishly enough, it has evolved as I have grown and matured. I'm sure that no one realizes I am no longer the little boy that doesn't want to do chores. After all, I still fuss and complain like that little boy. But now I complain because I am too smart and my work is too important to be delayed by taking out the trash or emptying the dishwasher.

I no longer need a robot to tackle the mundane for me. I need to fix so many of the things that are broken and not fair in the world. My reactor will allow me to bring power to any corner of the world. Imagine how lives can be changed and improved with unlimited free power!

After selling or licensing my design, I can use the profits to build reactors and travel to the places that will most benefit from the technology. My plan is to start in Ethiopia, where my brother Liam was born. Together we will travel to the village where his family lived and install the reactor. Refrigeration and electric water pumps will completely change the community. Instead of hours spent each day collecting food and water, they will be able to learn and think about the future.

After Ethiopia, I'll travel to China with my sister. She was born in a small city on the South China Sea but desperately wants to save the entire country. With pollution-free electricity, we'll be able to shift the base of control from the cities to the smaller villages and towns. People will flock out of the metropolitan areas where they are forced to wear masks and go days without sunlight because of the smog. They will need to rent or buy from the current occupants and it will be a seller's market.

My plans are big and far from selfish, but first I need to deal with my junior year of high school. I also want to keep an eye on this virus that seems to be getting out of hand. School I can deal with, even though it irritates me. The virus seems well beyond my control.

After eighth grade I asked my parents if I could take the GED and start taking classes at M.I.T. in the fall. Mom said yes and Dad said no. There was no doubt that I would pass the GED—I'm a genius, literally. There was also no doubt that I would be welcomed at M.I.T. I have been interacting with professors, PhDs, and doctoral candidates since the sixth grade.

Dad claims he was worried about my emotional development. He says that I wasn't ready, from a maturity-level standpoint, to attend classes with adults. He repeats, way too often: "Intellectual preparedness does not equal emotional preparedness." I think he was afraid of how much it would cost him for me to take classes.

They fought about it for maybe a week, but then the house needed a new roof and Liam needed braces. Necessities of parenting, home ownership and life came in and left me in my basement lab alone, solving not one, but two of the biggest physics questions of our time. How do you prove the existence of and identify a safe use for dark energy? All while fighting a daily battle with ignorant school administrators and under-educated and disinterested teachers.

On the other hand, there's the virus that seems to be sweeping around the world. They are calling it the "killer cold," an indiscriminate harbinger of death. I noticed activity spiking on Monday. "Fluid in the lungs" was trending as a Google search term and was also spiking on the global news feeds.

Mention of the "killer cold" was muted on establishment media outlets but there were references. The reports that were done tried to downplay the issue as a local, unfortunate series of unconnected deaths. Even a cursory review of social media topics and trends made it clear that the deaths were connected and not localized. I'm not sure where the virus came from but it is clear to me that no part of the world will be completely safe.

Today is Wednesday and I have survived another day of school. I was able to catch a nap in history class. We had a substitute and she played a movie. The other classes required that I keep my eyes open, but that was about it. There were several kids and teachers absent. Not enough to really worry anyone (other than me).

I wonder if I can convince Dad that we should all stay home for the next few days. Isolating ourselves from others who may be carrying the virus cannot be a bad idea. I'm sure he'll refuse, though, and tell me that when I have a temperature over 100 degrees I can stay home. He probably doesn't understand that this isn't a cold and you won't get better if you catch it. I don't have the energy to argue, though. My reactor is waiting, and once it's done all of these foolish discussions will come to an end.

Sometimes I wonder if I should have pursued medicine or biology instead of physics. With my intellect, I may have been able to cure diseases and save lives. Would I be able to understand and defeat this "killer cold"? Could I have made a difference in the world that way?

But I didn't *choose* to pursue physics. It chose me. When I first understood dark energy, it was just obvious. There were no classes or lectures that taught me how to understand particles, I just *knew*. I was frustrated that my choices for powering an autonomous robot were limited to tethering it to a wall socket or using AA batteries. My father's simplistic description of nuclear reactors and cold fusion sent me scrambling for Google.

That was my first all-nighter. I will never forget those agonizing hours spent lying in bed waiting for Mom to come upstairs. When she finally came up I waited not nearly enough minutes to be sure she was in bed for good. Then I was in the kitchen on the family computer. It was as if I was remembering things that I had been taught in a previous life. I *knew* how each of the reactions was going to play out and, more importantly, *why* they worked that way. I scared myself and to this day it sends a shiver down my spine.

Since that time I have been trying to explain to other physicists what it is I see and how I know it works. I'm working on an equation to describe what I know to be true, but that is no small feat. I feel strongly that I would rather complete my reactor to prove that what I know is true. Unfortunately, not everything is up to me. To get some of my resources, I have had to work with people and develop pieces of my equation. Some won awards and others didn't understand what I was showing them. Those that couldn't keep up would use my work in a thesis but break down during the defense.

CHAPTER 2

"Seamus, are you down there?" Dad's yelling from the top of the stairs interrupts me. I glance at the clock and see that it's already 6:10. Another sleepless night.

A deep breath. In the most measured tone I can muster I answer, "Yes Dad, I am."

He tells me to come up and get ready for school as if I had no idea that this is why he's yelling at me. School seems to be the most important thing in his world. Maybe it's second most important, just behind his routine. I hate school. In addition to boring me to sleep it has to be one of the most pointless institutions on Earth. My father thinks I say this because I'm sixteen. My mother knows I say this because, for me, it's true.

As soon as I reach the top of the stairs, the lecture begins.

"You know I don't like it when you sleep in your lab on a school night," Dad says with the stern *'I'm disappointed in you'* face he thinks is so scary. I can't believe he doesn't realize gym class is not a valid reason to delay my work.

"That's okay, I didn't sleep," I say, barely able to contain my smirk.

For someone who schedules and plans things down to the minute, my father never seems to see the details that matter.

"If you fall asleep again in history class, I may take away lab privileges for a week. We'll see how smart you are then." My dad is forever making threats. After sixteen years, I have long since figured out that he never follows through. It actually annoys me to no end. But somehow we have evolved into this dynamic. He has power over me by expressing his opinion and making empty threats. I know they are empty but I can't bring myself to push him only to prove that I know this. He should just say "Other people think I'm a bad parent when you fall asleep in public." As always, it seems obvious and simple to me. But the power is in his hands, and while I don't understand why, I respect it.

He knows that I don't need to go to school to learn what they teach in the classrooms. He says that for me school is about the social learning and finding a way to deal with a variety of personalities. If you are truly smart you can always learn from others, if you know what to look for. Apparently I don't know what to look for.

It's not like I don't have friends. Max and Alex are great guys and I can sit with them for a while talking about girls and video games. They don't even say anything now when I get up and leave in the middle of something to go home to my lab. But we're not what I would call "close."

The only place I am really happy is in my basement lab at home. Another knock on school, though—I built a physics lab in my parent's basement mostly using eBay and stuff I found at the dump. It is *way* better than what we have in school.

It's 2014 and the physics department in my high school, the best in the great state of New Hampshire, is still working with levers and ramps. I can learn from Google in five minutes what my physics class takes six weeks to cover. At home in my lab, work happens at the subatomic level—protons and neutrons. Hydrogen is my favorite element. It is so simple but carries so much power. Nevertheless, I have to sit through physics class and keep my mouth shut so the other kids have an "equal opportunity to learn."

It drives my mother crazy. From about the middle of

second grade she was asking why there wasn't a gifted program for me. The best schools in the state are not set up to handle the best students in the country. The schools should be forced to provide an educational challenge for me. But my parents have a weird dynamic. My Mom lets Dad manage the kids while she works to provide for the family. Dad doesn't want to rock the boat.

Mom is up this morning, which is weird. 6:20 a.m. and Mom almost never intersect. Must be a business trip.

"San Jose again?" I ask as she races about the kitchen. I am so much like her. Little things are stupid. Why can't someone else worry about getting the tools where they need to be? A surgeon doesn't pack, carry and keep track of all his instruments. His brain is occupied thinking about how the human body works so that he can use the tools to save a life. He stands over an open incision and calls out the tools he needs, which are then handed to him immediately and precisely.

Sure that she would agree with me but knowing it wouldn't help, I track down her phone and badge while she shoves her laptop, power cord and privacy screen in a bag. We both take the signature deep breath. No one else gets it.

She hugs me. "Thank you Seamus. You're always bailing me out." Not true but I don't protest. Maybe knowing that there is someone else in the world that sees how ridiculous it is to waste energy worrying about little things is what bails her out more than the locating of those little things.

"I know what you mean," I say, as Grace glides into the room.

Totally put-together and almost bouncing before 6:30 a.m., Grace is my polar opposite, yet we are halves of a whole. She keeps me grounded, sane. Grace is always there moments before I fly off the handle, and her presence keeps me in check. Her ability to diffuse my temper is magical. I love her so much; there isn't a thing in the world I would not sacrifice to protect her from sadness or discomfort.

Dad's making breakfast and packing lunches. I'm grateful

that he cooks and cleans for all of us, but really? How can an adult get satisfaction from so much time standing over the sink? It's not like he's Gordon Ramsey or anything, either. All winter it's baked or roasted protein, some tasteless vegetable, and noodles, rice or potatoes. He doesn't do big or extravagant, just enough to get by and a little better than takeout.

Liam rolls into the kitchen. He's a mess, totally disheveled, and he got a full night's sleep. Liam is off-the-charts different than Grace and me. Where I learn things and Gracie works hard at things, Liam just does things. If we were on an airplane and the pilot died, I could tell you how much lift each of the wings is able to generate, the horsepower of the engines, and, based on our altitude, the time left until we hit the ground with no pilot at the controls. Grace would download a manual and read frantically believing that she could learn to fly in time to save the plane. Liam would just walk to the cockpit, sit down and try to fly.

Liam asks why there is a limo in the driveway. For his ability to do things, he can't put two and two together. Even looking at Mom and her suitcase, he has to ask why there might be a limo in the driveway. But the car means it's time for all of us to get moving, the bus will be here soon, too.

Grace heads upstairs to brush her teeth and Dad grabs Mom's suitcase to take it out to the car. I'm on my way to my room when I hear Mom ask Dad if I was in the lab all night and what I might possibly be working on. Dad confirms that I was and he tells Mom that I am working on a battery or something. After that I am out of earshot and do not know what else they are talking about.

The truth is that it is not a battery. A battery stores energy and releases the energy until there is none left. Then you have to fill it up again. I am building a dark energy reactor. Even a small reactor will be able to generate hundreds of millions of watts of electricity. Even better, it will do so while generating no heat and requiring no catalyst. Well, no catalyst that we can notice.

Revolutionary new power reactor or not, I have to go to high school. There is a little excitement today but not the kind that I find interesting. The halls are at least half-empty, much worse than yesterday. Maybe it's senior skip day? Doesn't seem right for a Thursday in October. I'm dying to sleep, but I have English, history and gym this morning, which means no dozing.

When I finally get to physics class I am ready to shut my eyes and get fifty minutes of sleep. The teacher still thinks she can keep me engaged, so she has been starting classes off with interesting physics news from around the world. I try to humor her, but most of it is old news to me since I subscribe to the leading journals and am very much engaged with the global community online. But today she stuns me. A development in the concept of a solar sail has been published. A scientist in Australia claims to have proven that, using a new material, he can move a particle approaching the speed of light. I've read some on solar sails but not enough to be comfortable with them. What I do know is that the concept requires lots of power, like from, say, a dark energy reactor.

The power needed to catch and hold a single atom is massive. If I can get my reactor working, it might be able to generate enough energy to prove this concept in the real world. I don't understand why there are not more people working on the power piece of the equation. The solar sail theory is great and important, but if we can't move beyond simple nuclear reactors to generate power, we will forever be stuck experimenting and proving with equations. We need to increase our access to massive amounts of energy before we can move humanity to the next stage of evolution—interstellar travel. I guess I need to focus on my contribution first.

School is more of a nuisance than ever. It's all I can do to make it through the end of the period. I'm not even going to pretend that I'm sick. I just walk out of the building and start for home. My mind is racing. All the amazing people who said faster-than-light travel was impossible may be wrong. But I suppose there was a time when faster-than-sound travel was impossible, and a time when the earth was flat. It's almost as if the concept of "impossible" was created just so it could be proven wrong. I can't lose focus on my reactor, but I want to know more about this solar sail.

Dad's not home when I get there. He is probably out golfing or whatever. It doesn't bother me because it means I can go straight to the lab with no hassles about why I'm not in school.

The report is good. No, it's better than good. I would almost call it flawless. This guy did not want to publish until he was certain. I like that. Too many scientists lately have been publishing too soon, only to have their findings discredited. In some parts there is a feeling that rushing to publish is speeding along understanding. It gets more eyes on the idea and drives more detailed looks at advanced theories. It seems sloppy to me. There are even scientists who have built their whole reputation on disproving other people's work. Is this really science? These people have never had a creative thought in their lives, but they are process and documentation geeks. They will always find flaws in the way the people who do things actually do things.

Somehow the day is gone.

"Seamus, dinner time," Dad calls down from the top of the stairs. He doesn't even ask if I'm down here anymore; he knows. But still, I can't believe dinner is going to interrupt my work. If this solar sail theory holds up, we're probably five years away from having speed-of-light technology that will allow us to travel to another universe, and Dad wants me to put that on hold for grilled chicken and "the last of the season's tomatoes."

But I know what he would say. It's not about the chicken or tomatoes. *"It's about the family, we need to stick together. Who knows when we will need each other?"* I know he's right. Dad has worked so hard to help me get and keep friends. And I need friends. I want friends. But there aren't enough hours in the day. Half of one hour for family is what I can spare.

As we finish up dinner, the kitchen screen lights up. Must

be Mom skyping from California. Liam walks over to answer and immediately starts to tell Mom about how bummed he is that Saturday's soccer game was canceled because of so many kids being sick. They think they could have enough people to play, but they don't want to get everyone together and spread germs.

Grace thinks this sickness thing is a joke, *we* all feel fine. Together we've hypothesized that thanks to big media the entire world is having the opposite of a placebo effect. People think they are sick because the news has been talking about how many people are sick. I know it is real, but I want to shield her from the awful news.

Mom laughs when Grace tries to share our theory on the fake sickness, but she isn't buying it. The person she flew out to California to meet is too sick and the meeting will have to wait until Monday. She is not going to make it home for the weekend. That's a bummer. It's not like we spend a lot of time together or have special things planned, but it's always nicer when Mom is home.

Mom and Dad share some niceties while we do our chores. One of my earliest planned inventions was a robot that could do my chores. I wanted more free time. I was six—all I had was free time. But that one desire is what has driven me to this point. I realized that if I were to make a robot functional enough to learn and do chores, it would have to be small and have tons of processing power. This means lots of energy. Dad, who is forever thinking "in the box," pushed me toward a design tethered to a wall socket. But that just wouldn't do for something that was supposed to function somewhere between a puppy-dog and a servant. I started looking into fuel cells and innovative new power sources.

Power: my passion for the last eight years.

CHAPTER 3

Weekends are glorious. I think I finally went to bed around 4 a.m. on Friday night. Now it's about noon on Saturday. Dad has the screen in the kitchen on; must be a college football Saturday.

As I pour myself some orange juice, I realize that this is not the trivial sports contest I expected my dad to be watching. He has CNN on and is listening intently to the report. It seems I was right to be concerned about this virus. The newsreader is calling it an "epidemic" that they have been tracking for 48 hours, right after Mom left. I have been aware of the virus for a week. The last day, though, I have been so wrapped up in the solar sail theory that I forgot anything else was going on in the world. I wonder if the solar sail theory and the virus are somehow related.

There is a reporter on the screen that claims he went to a small town in Germany and found all the residents dead. Not one survivor. Then they cut to a doctor in a French town. He's standing on a country lane in what could be a Cézanne painting. But then he starts coughing. Between coughs, he says people from this area are dying fast. His hospital is full and he has taken to local airwaves to encourage citizens to stay home and die in the peace of their own beds.

Dad gives a weird chortle.

"I think the French get it. They don't confuse movement with progress." I'm not sure what he means. Does he mean don't fight death? Or does he mean that if you're ill you shouldn't try and get better?

"Dad, do you really think this is an epidemic that could wipe out the planet?" I ask, sounding more like an 8-year-old than I ever care to. "Should we just stay around the house today?" as if I had plans to go any further than my lab. "Is Mom going to be okay in California?"

"Why do you think it's going to wipe out the planet?" Dad asks, his face turning ashen. "Have you been looking into this and found something?"

"I'm asking. I have no idea if this is going to wipe out the planet." Why does he think that anything he doesn't understand has something to do with me? Just because I can figure things out does not mean I am an evil scientist.

"I'm sorry that came out like that. I'm scared," Dad says quietly as he tries to bring the tone down. "It's just that you figure things out faster than a lot of people. Sometimes you assume it's obvious to everyone and it's only clear to you. I thought that if you found something that could be helpful we should share it with someone."

So my dad thinks there is a viral epidemic that is going to wipe out the planet and his course of action is to sit in the kitchen and watch TV. Great, I feel safe.

"Dad, I have been reading a new paper on solar sails, I barely even noticed that people were getting this sick," I said, while realizing I need to start growing up a little. "Have you heard of anyone in Hollis dying?" I ask him.

"No, but it seems like the traffic is way down."

We both slowly make our way to the front porch where the rocking chairs are. We sit down and wait. When I was little, Dad, Grace and I would sit in these chairs and try to guess what color the next car was going to be. Dad and Grace could do it for hours. They never seemed to care if they were wrong. I could only play the game for a couple of minutes; it was pointless. There was no way to be good at it and no way to get better at it. But now there seem to be almost no cars at all.

After a few minutes, we walk back inside to the kitchen. The news anchor is reminding people to cough into their elbows and wash their hands. It seems a little pathetic. Dad shakes his head and says, "Something doesn't seem right about this." Then he walks out of the kitchen.

I am already on my way to the lab. I would rather bury myself in work than think or talk about feelings. Before I can get to the door, the screen beeps, signifying a video call. I want to ignore it, I know its Mom. What if she's sick?

Before Dad can get to the screen to answer, I walk-run over and click "answer." Mom's face fills the screen and lights up when she sees it's me who answered. Making someone else feel good makes me so happy, but I didn't really do anything. This is what Dad says I need to learn from school: people. Mom isn't the only one who likes to see me, but I spend too much time stressed out about why people like me. What do I do or need to do so they keep liking me? When I try and talk about it, they say, "Just be yourself." My self worries about what to do so people like me. But I don't want to do anything just because other people want me to do it. Being yourself is really hard.

"Hi Mom. How are you feeling?" I ask, dreading the moment when she coughs and gives me the sad knowing smile of impending death.

"I miss you guys. But I have a few books to read and I got some snacks yesterday. I think I'll make this a jammy day and read in bed until my eyes bleed." No cough.

How can such an intelligent person get so wrapped up in trashy vampire novels? Do they stimulate her creativity or are they just an escape from the world? Mom is brilliant; I know I get my intelligence from her. Is reading how she copes? Sometimes I have trouble shutting my brain off when I am thinking about something. It wouldn't surprise me if she has the same issue and uses fiction to get to a quiet space. Maybe once my reactor is complete I can start reading more. I would be happy to be more like Mom in every way.

"Hey babe," smiles Dad as he finally gets to the kitchen. "Are you going to have a jammy day or do you have work to get done?" Absent is any hint of concern in either of their voices. Does not knowing whether the person you love is going to die make it easier when they die? Or maybe they don't love each other? Or maybe they know each other so well that they don't need to ask the deep questions. I can't figure out relationships, and I'm not ready to try. At least not now; I've been given my cue to leave.

I spend most of the daylight in my lab. Dad keeps the screen off all day and stays busy outside.

It's puzzling that I share DNA with him. I cannot think of a trait that we have in common. Grace and Liam have no biological ties to him but have personalities that are almost direct derivatives of his. The three of them work outside at mindless physical labor. They interrupt yard work with random bouts of football, Frisbee, croquet and swinging.

I get the vegetable garden. While I do not like vegetables, I have arrived at the point where I know the difference between an heirloom tomato fresh from our garden and a mass-produced tomato from the grocery store. The garden provides food and reduces costs—makes sense. But the flower beds full of mulch? Purely for aesthetics? Seems pathetic to me.

I can't resist checking on the epidemic. In the last six hours it has become apparent that this thing is under-appreciated, at least by the news stations. People everywhere are dying. In poorer countries where hygiene is a challenge they are going fastest. One estimate is that 80 percent of the population of Africa will be dead in the next 24 hours.

I can't find a prediction for 100 percent of humans dying, but it must be a possibility. Even statistically speaking, if 1,000 people survive the epidemic, you could say we had 100 percent population loss. Scientists shouldn't be afraid to speak the truth, but they hedge their bets too much.

Before bed, Dad has the screen on again. I stand behind him and watch as the pretty newsreader gravely warns people to stay home, cough into your elbow and wash your hands. After coughing herself, she forces a smile and says "The best doctors in the world are working on a cure right now. Officials assure us there is nothing to worry about."

My guess is she'll be dead tomorrow, along with about 7 billion other people.

CHAPTER 4

Sunday passed in a blur. I spent the day mostly sequestered in my lab. The "killer cold" gnawed at the back of my mind, but I was able to make some progress on my reactor.

Upstairs there was a lot of shuffling about. The TV never came on and there were some board games and music but it didn't sound like the fun I usually hear. Do they think the "killer cold" will stay away because they are ignoring it?

Now it's Monday morning at 6:00 a.m. and Dad is waking me for school. Almost comical, Dad and his intractable routine. The last news we heard was telling people to stay home and avoid the sickness, but not my dad. Unless the school calls to cancel classes, Dad expects his children to be ready for the bus on time.

By 6:30, Grace, Liam and I have eaten breakfast and pulled our backpacks together. Dad is rushing us out the door so we don't miss the bus that I have no doubt will not be coming. In the commotion, he fails to notice that not a car passes by.

Liam forgot something. His gym clothes probably, or maybe a pencil. I don't think he cares about school much more than I do. But he seems to love going, which is the opposite of me. Is he using school to learn the things he needs to learn societally accepted interaction skills like Dad says, or his he just

17

oblivious? Does this make him a "willing learner" who magically learns what he needs to from whatever situation he finds himself in? I guess that makes me the "reluctant learner" who can only learn things I want to learn in the way I want to learn them. I'm jealous and dismissive of him at the same time.

Finally "dawn breaks on Marblehead" and Dad starts to look at the road. He notices the complete lack of traffic. He stands there bewildered for a minute and Grace catches on too.

People are stupid. People don't listen to the news. When we have blizzards, hurricanes and lengthy power outages, we still see cars on the road, joggers, dog walkers, people of any kind. And somehow we all know. They aren't staying home to be safe or avoid something potentially inconvenient. They are dead or at home dying.

As Liam comes back through the door, Dad slowly sinks to the top step and sits quietly. Liam stops talking about whatever he was saying and we all silently sit together on the steps, watching nothing.

For the first time in my memory, my mind is completely empty. I'm not waiting to get away to somewhere else. I'm not thinking about how dumb other people are. I'm not frustrated with the simplicity I must sit through. I just am. And I am afraid. It is probable that everything I knew as fact two days ago is entirely different today. That is not even accounting for the fact that we can't be sure if Mom is alive or dead, or somewhere in between. Everything I knew is gone. It's wrong, but I feel excited by the opportunity, and petrified at the same time. I can focus on the things that really matter: friends, family and being a good person. My reactor can be important but not all-consuming. Finding Mom is more important. She has to be alive, and we have to be with her.

We sit like this for a long time. Not moving, not speaking.

Grace finally breaks the silence. "I guess there's no school today?" she asks.

"No school today, or maybe ever," whispers Dad.

After another moment of silence comes a wave of activity. We are all up and in the house. Dad is kind of in a daze. It's like when he gets drunk at a holiday party. There is movement with no urgency. Thoughts come out of his mouth but they have no importance. It seems he's worried about Mom even though we spoke to her yesterday and she is not sick either.

I want to go to my lab. Research in peace or maybe just escape the emotions. But I know we all need to see each other right now. As if being in sight of each other will keep us from getting sick and dying. So I sit at the keyboard in the kitchen, looking for a Facebook page, blog, Twitter feed, or something that will identify other healthy people.

Grace is on the phone. I hear her leave her first message, unclear on what to say or how to say it. None of us have ever thought about leaving a voicemail for someone who is dying or already dead. When do you learn the right way to do that? I'm worried that we will all know how before today is over.

"Hi Gramma, it's Gracie calling to say hi. We don't have school today and I thought that if you weren't busy I could come up and we could have tea." We all know it's Gramma's reading time. She should be sitting in her sunroom with coffee and a book, the phone right next to her. But Grace is talking to the machine that picked up instead of Gramma.

"She's probably in the bathroom, honey. She'll call back in a few minutes, I'm sure," Dad tells Grace. But he's not sure, and we all hear it in his voice.

Liam still hasn't "earned" a phone of his own, so he's on the house phone, calling friends. No answers. He's leaving uncharacteristically short messages. "Hi Jason, it's Liam. Call me if you want to hang out today." He's manages twenty calls in the time it would normally take him for two.

Dad is texting friends and leaving voicemails for his brothers and sisters. He's trying to use his standard; "It's Paddy just calling to check in. Call me back and let me know how things are going." But the fear in his voice scares me. He's not expecting callbacks. Which means he thinks our family, our DNA, can catch the "killer cold." He thinks we, those of us with him in this room, are going to die.

"Ryan?" I turn to see Dad's face light up as he connects

with his brother. "How are things in Groton? This cold thing is getting crazy, right?"

After a minute or two of listening quietly, Dad speaks again. "Okay, if you guys want to come up here and hang out, we are just laying low and would love to have you. I'll check in tomorrow and see how everyone is doing."

"Are they coughing?" I ask, since I am the only one not engaged with finding friends.

"Aunt Stacie and the twins have the sniffles, but they don't think it's this "killer cold." They are drinking organic vinegar and eating garlic. Uncle Ryan thinks they'll be better in a day or two." Dad relays the conversation he just had.

"Do you believe him?" I can't help but feel like it is a naïve point of view.

"Well we're not sick, so I'm not sure why we should assume they are." Dad does not want to doubt Uncle Ryan's prognosis.

I send two quick instant messages to users who are offline. Unlike Dad and my brother and sister, I have hardly any friends to worry about. It's a strange feeling, wishing that you had someone close to you so that you could worry about whether they were alive or dead. I should have made more friends when there were other people alive. Now that most of the world is dying or dead, I'm starting to see the value in friendship and human contact. But it's ironic. Even if I had 100 friends they wouldn't be calling to check on me. They would be dead.

"Dad, why haven't you called Mom?" I ask, accusingly. I desperately want to stop thinking about my own faults and failures.

"It's only five in the morning in California, I don't want to wake her," he answers without delay.

This is the most normal and controlled voice I have heard from him this morning. Maybe he has thought of calling her. Maybe that was the first text message he sent. But shouldn't he be worried about her? Did he speak with her yesterday? I'm frantically trying to remember the last time I spoke with her.

Was it Friday or Saturday? Did she cough? Was she getting sick? I'm not sure if I'm worried about her health or if I'm worried about what her health will indicate for mine.

Finally around 10, Dad is trying Mom on the phone. It keeps going to voicemail, and he is getting frustrated. Sometimes Mom will forget that she needs to charge her phone and it will sit dead for days on end. This is a bad time for that kind of mistake, and Dad will be really angry if it turns out to be true.

"Let's pull the shades. I think we should lay low today. Oh, and can someone go around and check that the doors are locked?" says Dad quietly. Like when the neighbors lose power and we don't. Dad isn't comfortable making it obvious that we are okay and home. But why lock the doors? Could there be other people alive? What would they want from our house?

The emotions are too much for me. The others have all gone off to their quiet places, so I head to my lab. Now I'm kind of angry. I am so close to having this power reactor complete only to have this "killer cold" interrupt my work. This should be my dream day; Dad *asked* me to stay inside and lay low. I could spend 20 hours in my lab making progress, but I'm distracted. I just have to get working and see if I can lose myself. It's worked before, but I have never felt like this.

CHAPTER 5

I managed to get lost in my work. I just started a 4-hour test on my new containment field and glanced at the clock to see it's after 8 p.m. Dad never interrupted me for dinner—not good.

I make my way upstairs to find the screen in the kitchen on but blank and Dad sitting at the table with a glass of wine.

"No word from Mom yet," he says without looking at me.

"Do you want me to find the news?" I have nothing better to say to him. I have no more of an idea than he does if Mom is okay or if she died quietly, alone in a hotel in California.

"There is no news. Seamus, everyone is dead. As far as I know, we are the only humans alive on Earth." We haven't left the house in two days. How can he possibly know that no one else survived? It certainly feels that way, but there is no way it can be true. There *have* to be other people alive.

I stare blankly at the screen as if there might be an answer there. I feel powerless all the time, but this is different. Now I *am* powerless. I can't go anywhere or do anything to change the situation.

Suddenly I'm nervous that Grace and Liam might be sick and in bed. "Dad, where are Grace and Liam?"

"I think they are in the family room watching a movie. We thought it might take their mind off the waiting for someone to call," he answers mindlessly.

I walk to the family room, listening. Expecting to hear a cough or a sniff or some other sign that my sister and brother will be the next to die. But all I hear is the movie. I hear a laugh track, but not Grace or Liam. Maybe they are already dead.

Stepping around the coffee table I slowly look back at the couch, dreading what I expect to find.

"Could you move? I can't see the screen," says Liam. He has mastered the annoying little brother voice and it grates on me. A second ago I thought he was dead and, whatever I might have been feeling, I felt it down to my shoes. Now I'm kind of pissed that he's alive.

"Seamus, will you sit and watch with us?" Grace asks. I see her tear-stained face from the pile of blankets she's erected in her own makeshift shelter from bad things. I can't help but sit down next to her. She is too sweet to ever be in pain or fear. Grace has cried during movies before. She cries during scary movies, dramatic movies and almost always Gracie will even find a point to cry in funny movies. But I know this is different. The movie is just white noise. Everyone's mind is elsewhere. Well, maybe except Liam's, I think when he laughs loudly at the next funny part of the movie.

"What was that movie we saw for your birthday?" Liam asks. We've been to the movies for my last seven birthdays, so he's not really narrowing anything down for me. This is how he is.

"I have no idea what you are talking about," I say, but this is our dynamic, so he is already adding useless details that he knows will jog my memory. The fact is, though, that I was able to make the connection with the way his mind works. He's thinking about "The Hunger Games," which we saw for my thirteenth birthday.

Now my mind is racing again. Government-controlled rations, government-controlled health stasis. Could this "killer cold" have been created by the government as a weapon? Is it being unleashed only on the states that do not support the current president? He would have plausible deniability and the states that support him would never question the truth. It seems vaguely possible. We don't know anyone in the Midwest or middle America. Everyone we are trying to connect with is on one of the coasts. The liberal coasts. Of course, with New England and California gone, the United States is left with the "strong American heartland." The bulk of the population is erased, and all that is left is hard-working Republican farmers.

The phone rings. It scares us all, but there is no movement. I don't know how much wine Dad has had but I know he'll answer. I'll have to come back to my conspiracy theory later.

"Ryan calm down. Let me come pick you up, it'll be okay," Dad says into the phone as he walks into the family room.

The BANG is audible through the phone. Dad yells "NO!" but it's a futile gesture. Uncle Ryan is dead. He was a really great uncle, but right now I'm not sad.

"Dad, was he coughing?"

"No. He was fine. Healthy like us," he says, followed by a long silence.

"Aunt Stacie and the twins were sick yesterday. They died this morning some time. But Uncle Ryan was fine. He was just sad. He loved them so much he didn't want to go on without them." Dad is staring out the door, talking to himself, mostly. There was another adult close by that he knows and cares about and who survived the "killer cold"— but now he's gone.

The "killer cold" did not affect my dad and Uncle Ryan. I share some of their DNA, so I am optimistic about my chances. I wonder if Grace and Liam think about their chances for long-term survival.

Grace was born in China to parents she never knew and has no way to trace. For all we know, they could also be alive. Or they could have died years ago in an accident, from cancer or starvation. I wonder if this has an effect on her outlook for life. She has always been able to just deal with things the way they are. It's not ignorance or acceptance; more like understanding. But she never dwells on anything or lets what could have been affect her dreams or goals. I think that if she isn't sick now she will survive.

Liam is in a similar but different situation. He knew his first family in Ethiopia, his parents, his sisters and his aunt. He was young but somewhere in his brain he must remember their faces and voices. He also knows that his parents passed away years ago. Their deaths were listed as "high blood pressure" and "weak heart," which are pretty general descriptions. His extended family tried to keep him but could not. They barely had the resources to provide food for themselves. His relatives may have survived, but how can we ever get in touch with them? There are no phones in their village, so we are left to wonder.

"Do you think there are other people out there who didn't get sick?" Grace asks.

"Let's go drive around and see if we can find other survivors," suggests Liam.

"No. It's late and dark, I don't want to leave the house right now. We'll go out tomorrow." Without another word Dad is on his way to the kitchen, probably for more wine. I guess he deserves it.

Grace and Liam return their semi-focus to the movie but my mind is off again.

What if there are government agents patrolling the streets looking for survivors so they can eliminate them? Even if it is less sinister and they are looking to capture survivors to run tests and experiments on to find a cure, I'm scared. Would the scientific community sacrifice a family to find a cure for a larger portion of the population? Probably. Would they ask the family for permission? Probably not. I'm starting to think that this is not going to end well for me. Maybe catching the "killer cold" would have been preferable to what lies ahead.

Again my thoughts of conspiracy are interrupted. This time it's the phone buzzing. Dad never hung up after the call with Uncle Ryan. But Grace is up and straightening things in the family room. It's no surprise that she has pulled herself together. Silently she crosses to the phone and hangs it up. As if related and on cue, the screen from the kitchen chimes to indicate an incoming Skype call.

The Skype call is not answered immediately and Grace heads to the kitchen to see if Dad is still in there. After a minute the chiming stops and I hear Grace shout with joy. "Mom!"

We are all very happy to have Mom on screen and not only talking with us but also looking at us. Grace tells her that we did not go to school today. Liam shares that one of the chickens looks like she lost some feathers and I ask about her flights. Not only was she not able to reschedule, they weren't even answering the phones at the airline. We are all aware of the extent of the death in the world, but it still hasn't sunk in that this changes the way things work. I don't know where he was, but Dad finally comes into the kitchen to join the conversation.

"Any luck with the flights?" he asks casually.

"No. But there is something I want to talk with you about," Mom answers, and looks at us kids like she does not want to speak while we are present.

"Guys, could you excuse us?" Dad says to all of us, but looks directly at me.

We all say goodbye to Mom, but none of us leave the kitchen. There is awkward silence all around. We are all practically adults; they should let us in on whatever is going on. In the new world, we need to be aware of everything. I look over at Grace and see a tear streaming down her face.

"When are we going to see you again? I don't like you being in California; I want you here with us!" Grace is speaking louder than normal but only to fight through the tears.

Liam is crying too, but silently. "I love you, Mom," comes out, barely audible.

"I can't deal with all of them by myself, Mom. I need you with us so everything works right." I'm trying to be funny but I want to burst out in tears. I don't *want* Mom to be okay, I *need* her to be okay.

"I love you all so much." It's Mom's turn to cry. "I

promise that I will be all right and we will all be together soon."

After some more tears and "*I love you*'s" we three kids turn to head back to the family room and resume the movie. Grace and Liam don't pause in the door and head right for the couch. I wait just past the doorway, knowing from experience that you can hear the conversation from here but not be seen by either party. It's wrong for me to listen in, but we are not planning a birthday party here.

"Paddrick, you need to get out here right away." I hear Mom's voice; it is on the verge of tears.

"I'm planning the drive out there now. I'm a little nervous that some parts of the country did not get the virus at the same time as us. If there are groups of survivors left, they may be violent." Dad never says he is afraid but that's the message he is sending.

"We have a vaccine for the virus. If you don't get out here right away you will all die!" Mom is yelling and breaks down into tears.

"What do you mean *we*?" Dad sounds stunned and instead of focusing on the life-saving vaccine, he is wondering whether or not Mom is alone.

"I met a couple of physicists at a Starbucks when I was searching for coffee. They work at some government installation in Palo Alto and they have a vaccine. Why are you arguing with me?! Get my children out here immediately!" Mom may be experiencing a breakdown of sorts.

"Okay, Okay," Dad pauses to think about what he has to say next. "I need some time to get things together, this won't be an easy trip." He waits for a long time. "We'll leave as soon as we can."

"Make sure that Seamus brings his reactor work. The vaccine needs to be refrigerated and we are already having rolling blackouts." Mom looks uneasy before she continues. "Paddrick, I'm sorry I never told you. But the whole family has already received the vaccine. You need a booster soon or -"

When did we receive the vaccine? The screen went dark

before Mom could finish speaking. I've stepped into the kitchen, no longer concerned with listening in secret. Dad is leaning on the chair in front of the screen as if the weight of the world is crushing down on his shoulders. He is not crying but he may not be breathing either. I walk over and place my hand on his back, unsure of my role in this situation.

Dad turns and hugs me in a strong embrace. We do not speak but remain like this for several minutes. He must be nervous and confused, but he is doing an amazing job of holding it together.

CHAPTER 6

Classic. For the first time in ages I don't *have* to go to school but I'm awake at 6 a.m. But how could anyone sleep? The apocalypse has come and gone. There was no nuclear war, no asteroid impact or other singularity. They couldn't have made a movie about this—it's too boring.

It's still a possibility that a government or rogue villain released a bio-weapon. If that were true, I would expect there to be someone else alive. Even megalomaniacs don't usually want to die themselves. If someone were to have done this on purpose, they must have wanted something. Now that Mom has revealed that there is a vaccine, and that there are others alive out there, it is clear that someone was involved.

In one of the "Star Trek" movies, Spock says that when you rule out all the possibilities, the impossible must be an option. There are so many possibilities I can't stand it. My focus has been about identifying and clarifying problems and then solving them. With this I can't really identify the problem, so how can I possibly solve it?

I've learned that this "killer cold" only infected humans. In searching for signs of other survivors, I encountered more than one blog post and YouTube clip that described basically the same thing. They would start coughing within about twelve

K. D. McAdams

hours of contact with a carrier. Within 24 to 36 hours of contact, they would become lethargic. After giving in to the lethargy, it was relatively quick. If you sat upright, your lungs would fill with fluid and drown you in about ten hours. If you lay down it was much faster, four to six hours.

My guess is the virus began killing people some time last Tuesday and by the following Sunday 7 billion people were dead. Including the people in this house, Mom and the scientists in California, there are 7 people left on Earth. Statistically speaking, 100 percent of the human race is wiped out.

The scientific approach would be to figure out who was patient zero, the first person to be infected. But that is a pointless and impossible exercise. The right thing to do now is move on.

As of now I am considering yesterday Post-Apocalyptic Day one—PAD1. That makes today PAD2. If the post-apocalyptic world is going to be any good, I have to make today much better than yesterday. That shouldn't be hard. The first step is to get out of bed.

When I get downstairs, Dad is sitting on the screen porch with a cup of coffee and a legal pad. I guess it's a good sign that he's making a list of something. This is usually his precursor to actually doing things, a list. But when I look closely, it's a grocery list. Denial is not just a river in Egypt.

"Good morning, Seamus. There's coffee in the carafe." He acts like this is normal, but it's not. He never offers me coffee. He used to say, "It'll stunt your growth. When you're 18, you can decide for yourself. Until then I'm in charge, and I don't want you drinking coffee." He knows I drink it to stay awake when I am running tests in the lab. But he never lets me get a coffee when we are on road trips and he makes a stop for him and Mom. Dictator Dad is not cool. I'm not sure what it is I want from him, but this is a good first step.

"So, Dad, do we have a plan? Do we know what we are going to do?" I say, hoping the disgust on my face is apparent. The only thing I can think of him right now is "impotent."

"Well, we're not going to have electricity for much longer. And we need to eat. I want today to be all about getting provisions."

As if using the word "provisions" instead of "food" makes him something he could never be. A leader. A survivor. Someone in control of the situation. I laugh at the situation more than the answer. The only adult in my new post-apocalyptic world is working on his vocabulary instead of something that is going to help us.

"You know, Seamus, this isn't easy on me either. There is no rulebook or FAQ on how to survive an apocalypse," he says.

And he is suddenly in full lecture mode.

"When I was in high school, there was a player for the Bruins named Cam Neely. He was great. A forty-goal scorer, a big tough guy who could fight and grind it out in the corners. He was just an absolute all-star. But then he got hurt. And during the games the TV would show him up in the press box watching the game. The first few times he was restless -- you could tell he wanted to be on the ice. But then he started to watch the games more calmly, like he figured something out. When he came back from his injury, people were worried he wouldn't be the same. And he wasn't. He was better. After plenty of interviews, we all understood what he learned up in that press box. You have more time than you think. When it feels like you should be in a hurry, slow things down. Take your time and make smart, deliberate actions."

"Well I'm not sure how a hockey stick is going to get us back with Mom. But I can tell you one thing, Dad, this is not a game and there is no press box. You need to be a man and save our family." I'm surprised at my strength and how I challenge my father. But it feels good.

"Listen to me, Seamus. You may consider yourself unlucky that I am alive. But the fact of the matter is there are still people other than you in this world and we need to think about them, too. For some reason, our family was vaccinated and survived the apocalypse. I will not get us all killed by blindly charging off across the country." My father is standing over me now. Somehow he makes the two-inch difference in height seem like two feet. I regret challenging him, and now it feels the opposite of good.

He sits back down and picks up his legal pad. I have nothing to say and I can't seem to move. He's wrong. We need to leave today. My next move may set the tone for the rest of my life. If I sit down and drink coffee, I will forever be a child. If I walk out and head off on my own, I'll lose my whole family. Do I really want to be alone for the rest of my life? No matter how long or short it may be, this thought and my inability to decide has me frightened.

Finally my father gives me the out I need.

"Seamus, sit down. I need you. You are the smartest person I have ever met. We are going to have to figure out a lot of things in the next few weeks. If you can stay calm and stick with me, I will let you have complete freedom once we get to California," he says. He's somewhere between taking charge and just holding on. But right now, that's enough for me.

We sit in silence until Grace comes down a while later. She pours some orange juice and then walks out into the apple orchard and grabs a few apples. Dad and I both watch her without saying a word. She feels things deeper than the rest of us but she knows how to get on with things. There is nothing to talk about right now; she wants to eat. Dad and I could argue through starvation about what and how much to eat. Grace just eats.

When she comes back inside, Dad starts laying out his plan. But sadly it doesn't cover anything beyond today. He wants to spend the day getting supplies and collecting memories. This does nothing for humanity, but I know that in a few days we will be leaving New Hampshire forever. He can only be hoping for closure.

After Liam wakes up we all manage to pull ourselves together and take showers and eat some food. The sit-tight plan still bugs me but I am able to shelve my frustration for the time being.

"Let's mount up. We need to go to Wal-Mart and a few other places before it gets dark." This is how Dad talks when we don't have the option of not going with him. Still, I protest.

"I'm going to stay home," I say as I head towards my lab.

But Dad stops me. "No, Seamus, we are sticking together for the next couple of days."

Grace and Liam wait intently to see what I am going to do. I can see no point in fighting Dad on this. Besides it might be interesting to drive around and see if there are any other survivors.

As soon as we are on the road, I regret coming. We are going to Grandma's house. This reminds me that she and Papa are dead. I don't want to think about that, but now I can't think of anything else. I imagine them lying next to each other in bed holding hands, probably even smiling. They had fifty years together and they knew how lucky and wonderful they were. Seeing them in any way other than peaceful would ruin me.

When we get to their house, we sit in silence for a minute. Then Dad makes us all go in. He wants us each to collect a few of our favorite memories of them. At first it's awkward and difficult, but soon we start talking and laughing. We're gathered in the kitchen like always. There are two dead people in the next room, but we are flooded with good memories of holidays and visits here. Finally I share with Liam and Grace how I picture them in death. I'm not conscious of it, but I know Dad is nearby listening.

I'm not sure how long we spend in their house. When we leave, each of us is happy to let my vision be the reality of their final rest. We didn't really take that much, but I realize the memories in our heads are what Dad wanted us to hold onto.

The ride to Wal-Mart is short but quiet. The experience at Grandma's house is preventing me from processing how eerie things are with no people around. In the parking lot, Dad has us each grab a cart and tells us to follow him. We're just moving now, no thoughts or feelings, simply motion.

"Dad, why are we going to the guns section?" Grace does not like guns. "We need to stop and get food. Mom wouldn't want us to have guns."

"We all need to learn to use and be safe around guns now. They will become a constant in your life so get used to it." Dad is not usually this abrupt with Grace.

I want to ask him if these will be for hunting or protection but I don't. The only logical answer is both. Grace does not need to be aware of the concept that "bad guys" may be out there and ready to hurt us. For me, I am aware that "bad guys" could mean government agents, a paramilitary group or even aliens. I'm not comfortable with guns but I am open to their value.

It's a quick, efficient stop. Dad makes fast work of the necessary but unpleasant task of arming ourselves. We load up with eight weapons: four shotguns and four rifles. Dad wants a sidearm but this Wal-Mart does not seem to carry handguns. I guess there will have to be another stop. My shopping cart is full of the guns and the ammunition they use. Grace is too afraid to put them in her cart and Liam... well let's just say we're not comfortable with him holding a gun.

Getting food and sleeping bags is a little easier. Grace fills her cart with dried food like Ramen Noodles, rice and beans. Liam is in charge of canned goods. Dad puts things like snacks and drinks in his cart. We each have a nice new sleeping bag tucked into the bottom of our cart. With the exception of the cart full of weapons and ammo, it looks as if we are getting ready for a beach party.

"Hold on, I'll be right back," Liam is yelling as he runs away. Dad is not happy but we wait patiently.

"Got it," Liam says, as he finally comes around the corner. He's holding a can opener. We know there is one at home but we all feel like this is a brilliant thought. Liam is smiling triumphantly as we head for the exit with our loaded carts.

CHAPTER 7

Post-apocalyptic etiquette is still largely undefined. Dad parked in a parking space just like he would have a week ago. For a moment I feel so superior to him for realizing that he could have just pulled up on the sidewalk right in front of the door. In fact, he probably could have driven right through the doors and parked in the produce section.

I come down to Earth a little bit when I realize that this thought is only now entering my mind. When we got here and he pulled into that spot, it felt like the most natural thing in the world. I was grateful that he didn't park far away and tell us to walk because we needed the exercise. I need to lighten up on the old man a little.

At the car, we realize that packing all this stuff and getting the four of us home is going to require a little planning. Dad folds the seats down in the back of the van and it creates plenty of room. I'm loading the guns and ammunition in first. We don't need them right now; they weigh a ton and they can't get crushed.

As I grab the last shotgun I am aware for the first time of the tractor-trailer trucks in the parking lot. There are always a few present based on Wal-Mart's policy of supporting truckers and campers' overnighting, but this seems like a lot.

I'm counting the trucks while laughing at the fact that I have no basis for how many trucks were typically there when I see the RV. It seems strangely out of place, and I can't help but stare at it for an extra minute. While I'm staring, the door opens and a girl walks out. Maybe it's a woman. Whatever; another human being, definitely female.

"Dad," is all I can manage to say.

"Unh huh," is his response, somehow making it clear to me that he sees her, too. But I'm scared, because his first reaction is to grab one of the shotguns and load it with several rounds. Why is he assuming danger? The concept of zombies or mutated humans who only want to eat survivors is ridiculous.

She's walking towards us and it is clear that there is no danger around her. Wearing a skirt and thin blouse with sandals on her feet, there is no place for her to conceal any type of weapon. I hope Dad keeps that shotgun in the back of the van.

As she gets even closer, I can see that she is beautiful. Not supermodel or famous-actress beautiful, but simple, girl-next-door beautiful. The kind of girl who doesn't wear makeup, because she never thought to, not because she is trying to make a statement or have a "signature style".

My heart is fluttering and my mind is racing. Thoughts of other survivors have been men in black jump suits with submachine guns. Bad guys dominate my perception of post-apocalyptic world survivors. This is unexpected and very much welcome, except for the fact that I am thrown off balance. This almost never happens to me, even when the prettiest girl in school would sit next to me in class or at lunch, I was never fazed by it. Now, I'm mush.

As she gets close enough to speak, I'm telling myself to pull it together. I'm almost composed when she smiles. My knees go weak and I'm speechless. But not Liam, he's right there and already being Liam.

"Hi, is that your motorhome?" Liam asks her. The first survivor we have met and Liam wants to know about the motorhome.

"Yes, it's my parents'. Or, it was. I guess it was theirs." She trails off.

"Cool, can we go inside?" Liam carries on. I'm not sure if he is aware that most of humanity has been wiped out or if he is consciously trying to keep things normal.

"Well, it's pretty messy and I don't think you want to see it like that," she says, but she's stopped walking. This other survivor, this beautiful girl, is standing about 6 feet away from us. Further than you would in a normal conversation, but closer than she probably should for her own safety, not knowing us and all.

"Oh, well, messy..." Liam starts in.

"Liam," Dad silences him.

"Are you from around here?" Dad asks in a tone somewhere between grouchy cop and indifferent schoolteacher. I'm not sure why it matters. If she lives in the town over do we help her, and if she is from far away, leave her? A better question is probably about her ancestry to see if we can start to figure out a DNA combination that survived this thing. But Dad is probably still trying to figure out what to do.

The only pick-up line I have ever given credit comes into my mind. I blurt it out without even thinking. "Hi, my name is Seamus."

The smile is back and she is walking closer to us. "My name is Sofie. I am so happy to see other people that are alive!" Then she is hugging me and crying and laughing. It feels so good to hold her. But my brain is conflicted. She should feel so good to be alive. Who cares about seeing other people? Worry about yourself.

Until now, I haven't even thought about what it would be like to go through this alone. What if I had cared for Dad, Grace and Liam as they progressed through coughing into drowning in their own fluids and then death? Would I have carried their bodies out to the back yard and buried them? Would I have left them where they lay and gone off in search of something? How would I have handled it?

For all the times I yelled that I want to be alone or told people to leave me alone, I have never been alone. The few times I have had the chance to be left alone for more than a couple of hours, Grace or Liam have been there, and I didn't want or ask them to leave. Now the thought of being alone frightens me, and I shudder a little as we break our embrace.

The sound of a shotgun loading snaps me back to reality. Dad is not as relaxed as the rest of us. He doesn't seem concerned with Sofie but I can tell by his eyes that he thinks something is fishy with the trucks and even Sofie's motor home.

Without looking at her, Dad asks, "Sofie, was there anyone in that motorhome besides you?" Now we're all staring, as if looking at the motorhome will give us an answer.

"Just my parents," she says softly. The way she says it makes me understand that they are dead and will not be walking out the door.

I wish Dad would communicate and tell us what he is looking for, what he is thinking or what he is afraid of. If he thinks he's doing strong silent type, he's wrong. Suddenly I wonder if he's trying to impress Sofie. Mom is alive in California; he's not free to date just because of the apocalypse. Or maybe Mom isn't as okay as we thought. Maybe we'll get a sit-down tonight and Dad will break the bad news to us. Telling us he didn't want us to worry. There's one eligible girl left in the world and I have to compete with my Dad and Liam for her attention. But I got the hug.

Somehow satisfied that zombies, commandos or mutant dogs aren't going to be coming out of the tractor-trailer trucks, Dad is ready to move on.

"Grace, why don't you and Sofie go gather her things from the motor home. Seamus, if there is anything you need for your lab or to get the power pack working sooner rather than later, go get it now. Liam will go with you. I'll load the car. I want to leave in fifteen minutes."

CHAPTER 8

It took another 45 minutes for us to leave Wal-Mart. Dad never could stick to his own time restraints. We never really talked about Sofie coming with us or if she even wanted to. She just got in the van and road silently home with us. The count of survivors that we know about is at eight and I'm thinking about a spreadsheet to keep track of people.

Dinner was strangely silent but bland as usual. Dad offered Sofie the guest room, but she chose to stay on the trundle bed in Grace's room. Everyone was moving about in a daze. I couldn't motivate myself to even go into my lab, let alone sit and work. I'm not sure why, but I kind of thought we would celebrate when we found another survivor. Instead, we all just sort of shuffled off to our rooms and went to bed.

Once again I'm wide awake at 6 a.m. I don't want to get out of bed today. I don't want to "sit tight" for another day. But I don't want to fight with my Dad in front of Sofie. I don't know how to impress her, but I'm pretty sure that acting like a spoiled teenager won't do the trick. Every time I try and switch my brain over to the reactor, Sofie's face shows up. The flow of electrons that is usually so clear to me is interrupted by memories of the hug. A girl preoccupies me and it feels good. But I have work to do, so it is insanely frustrating.

I must have drifted off to sleep. When I look at the clock again, it's 7:20, so I roll out of bed.

Dad is alone in the kitchen, but not like usual. He's not sitting with his cup of coffee and reading or making a list. There are sheets of legal paper on the island arranged neatly, each with a bold headline and a string of numbers on the left edge. While we have five iPads and three laptops in the house, Dad is using a Sharpie and legal pad for his notes. But he's moving with a purpose, so I won't nitpick.

"Good morning, Seamus. I'm glad you're up." He's said this before. This time it's different, though, not like, *"I love you, son."* It is more like when he would say good morning to my uncles on holidays.

"I spoke with Mom last night and she wants to make sure you guys know she's okay," he starts. I guess I don't get offered coffee this morning. Maybe I should just pour some without commenting. When we were little, he used to tell us, "When you act like a big kid I'll treat you like a big kid." So I decide to act like an adult from here out, and pour myself some coffee.

I sit at the island and ask, "Are there any other survivors out there?" trying my best not to be emotional and act differently, even though I know things have changed.

"No. But I want to talk about the plan before the others get up. I'm going to need your help if we are going to make it across the country alive." He's shuffling papers around but looking at me intently.

"Let me know what you need me to do," I answered, out if instinct, full of confidence but clueless as to how to proceed.

"You have one day to get your power reactor functional. At some point we are going to need power that's not on the grid and I want you to be ready when that time comes."

"It doesn't work like that Dad. I just had my first successful test of the containment field on Monday. I'm estimating weeks before I'm even ready to test power generation." I hope that isn't whiny, just factual.

"Well tomorrow we're packing up to leave. We hit the

road at daybreak on Friday."

The expression and tone make it clear to me that this is a timeline that won't budge. It's not the parking lot at Wal-Mart. I'm desperately hoping he doesn't say that he's leaving with or without me. I don't need an ultimatum and I can't imagine being left alone.

"Do whatever you can to make progress and have your work as portable as possible. We won't have a lot of space, but we'll pack as much of your lab as we can." Dad is making exceptions for me. I've never felt this kind of support for my work before.

"The shopping spree at Wal-Mart was nice, but it didn't actually help that much. What I really need is to go to Stellos Electric and BAE to find some things that will really help," I say, not sure if I'm sounding optimistic or just hopeful.

"Fine. When Liam wakes up, take him and the van and go get what you need. But stay together." Dad's made a decision and we're moving on. *A brave new Dad*, I think to myself as I recall a literature assignment that was given but never completed.

"According to Google Maps, it's about 50 hours from here to San Mateo, where Mom's hotel is." Dad is referencing his sheet of legal paper with the heading *Plan*.

"I don't want to do too much driving at night, so I'm guessing the best we can do is 12- to 14-hour days. That puts us in there sometime Monday."

I'm not sure if he wrote all this down or if he has a bullet point to spur his memory.

"Do we have to follow the speed limit?" Realizing I should ask a better question about halfway through my verbalization of the lame one, I try again: "I mean, I think we can make it in three days. Google Maps assumes that we're going sixty-five or maybe even fifty-five. We can probably average 100 to 110 with no other cars on the road."

"Good point. The sooner we get there, the better. If we get there Sunday, I'll be happy. But we should probably factor in some time for the unexpected. Being late is a lot worse than being early for worrying your mother. Let's communicate the plan for arriving Monday and we here can know that Sunday is doable."

I can tell Dad hadn't thought of this since he wasn't looking at his paper when he said it. He's adapting to my input on the fly and we aren't fighting about it. I hope this dynamic can continue.

"What are Liam and Grace going to do while I am working on my reactor?" If Dad is going to let me in on the plan, I want to know as much as I can.

"I'm going to have Grace and Sofie go to the Historic Society and some of the neighbors' houses. I want them to build a small history chest of this area. There may not be humans here again for hundreds of years. When they arrive I want them to know about the people that inhabited this space."

It's somber and eerie but my dad is right to leave some sort of reminder.

"Make sure you leave a note that makes it clear this wasn't a war or anything man-made that wiped out the population. I don't want the future to think that we were animals." I can't believe how emotional and sensitive this feels. It really matters to me. Only after the silence do I realize that we should also comment on the virus in case they need to find a cure for it themselves.

The silence is awkward and long. I wonder if this is how it is going to be every time we talk about the virus.

"What about Liam?" I ask, ready to move on before my father.

"Liam is going to be muscle today," Dad says, knowing it sounds mean but comfortable with his decision.

"You know he is smarter than you give him credit for," I say, not sure if Dad and I are at the point where I get to give the lectures.

"Well, you know better than anyone what happens between you two when he gets going and spins his energy up. Both of you spiral out of control fast, and the last thing I need right now is a fight."

But I barely hear him say these last words.

I have an idea. It could be just what I needed to complete the reactor. If can shape the containment field into an ever-shrinking spiral, like a snail shell, this will accelerate and compress the anti-matter and have it reach the core at full potential energy. Power comes out one side of the core and waste out the other.

I need to go to the lab and draw a picture so this thought doesn't disappear. But Liam and Grace are shuffling into the kitchen. I want to be here when Dad explains the plan. It will help me seem like a co-creator and give me some authority.

"Morning, Dad," says Grace.

"Oh, yeah. Morning, Dad," says Liam, like he forgot it was morning or that this is what we say to each other every morning of every day.

"Can I get you two some breakfast?" The old Dad is back. I didn't notice him clearing the counter, but his papers are gone. I guess being on the adult team means I have to get my own breakfast. Or maybe this is his subtle payback for all those mornings I didn't acknowledge him and went straight to my lab. I don't really feel like eating anyway.

"I have something I need to try in the lab. Liam, can you come get me in an hour? And don't let me say no. We have to go get a few things and I really need your help." That wasn't very hard. My parents have been trying to get me to communicate little things like this for years. It doesn't take any brain cycles, but I still don't really see the point. I guess it makes the other people feel good about what I am doing? I wish they wouldn't care what I was doing though. But that's the old world, this is PAD-3 and I am on the adult team.

The hour goes by too fast. I want to tell Liam to go away and give me a little more time. Why is he so annoying? I've reconfigured the containment controller to create a circular shape. I just need another twenty minutes or so to add the logic for spiraling near concentric circles. But I remember telling him not to take no for an answer. I'm on the adult team and I have to avoid confrontation, so I save my work and head upstairs.

In my brain, the reactor is done and functional. I can see the anti-matter reaction and the flow of electrons, neutrons and protons. I know this is going to work as soon as I can finish the task of physically implementing my design. The problem I am trying to solve now is making the power output usable in today's world.

Current power plants have multiple output channels. Each of these channels, in turn, goes to a power substation where it is run through meters, inductors and transformers. Then it heads out on the wire to its final destination. My reactor doesn't have multiple channels out, just one. That one channel has the power equivalent of 1,000 power plants. I had always assumed that after I released my design there would be people lining up to help me solve this last problem. Now I have to solve it if we are going to survive.

Thinking about controlling power is helping me with Liam right now.

"We have to go to Stellos Electric and BAE. Do you want to drive?" I already know the answer is yes. Liam has moved from "muscle" to driver. In his mind, it's probably assistant or even co-inventor for my reactor, but I don't care.

"Can we take the Cayenne?" Liam says before he turns to walk towards the keys.

"No. Besides making Dad angry, it doesn't have the cargo capacity of the van." I've just realized the point about cargo, but it makes it seem like Dad and I discussed this and we had a plan.

Before we walk out the door, Grace and Sofie come into the kitchen. They are both dressed in yoga pants and sports bras. I absentmindedly sit down at the table. I have seen Grace in her workout clothes a thousand times. From the dozens of guys that ask me about her, I know she is cute. But she is my sister so I don't really see it. Sofie, on the other hand, is stunning.

Smooth is not in my repertoire. I know this because Liam

is talking with Sofie and they are all looking at me now. Someone must have asked a question. Not only do I not have the answer, I can't even guess at the question. And I'm probably staring.

"Do you guys want a ride?" Maybe having power over the car will give me some coolness.

"No. Seamus, I asked if you knew where Dad is," Grace is looking at me with her amused *you need to pull it together* face.

I'm still sitting down and realize that I look foolish, but I'm regaining my faculties.

"I don't know where Dad is, but I'm pretty sure he didn't have exercise in the plan." Now I'm getting my swagger.

"Seamus, Dad told me the plan. Sofie and I are going to walk to the Historic Society. If we are going to be cooped up in a car for four days, I want to get some exercise and fresh air now." Grace does not acknowledge any swagger. "I wanted to tell him we were leaving so he would know where we are. Will you tell him we left?" she says over her shoulder as she and Sofie head out the door. They have known each other for less than 24 hours but have been talking like they were friends for life. I don't understand how they can have so much to say.

"Come on, Seamus." Liam is out the door and wants to drive.

I get up from the chair and follow after him. I'm not really sure where we are going or what materials I wanted to source. I hate struggling with things that are not scientific. When there are no facts, there is usually no point, as far as I'm concerned. But my feelings for Sofie have no facts. I can't rationalize them with a formula. For some reason I just want to catch up to them and walk beside her and listen to what she and Grace talk about. But that would be pointless.

In a fog, I climb into the van and tell Liam we're good to go.

CHAPTER 9

Dad was *pissed* that we didn't leave a note or some other method of telling him we had left.

We all get a stern lecture about communicating. Sofie is spared a little bit, but Dad makes it pretty clear that if she is going to stay with us she will be held to the same standard. I am a little surprised at how she handles him. She offers a simple, honest apology and an acknowledgement that there is one set of rules for everybody.

Grace tries to explain to Dad that everyone makes mistakes, including adults. But that isn't what he wants to hear. He calls it backtalk and makes clear that this is not what he expects from his children. I see only a subtle difference between what Grace and Sofie said and I want to argue details and stick up for Grace. But I hold my tongue; the sooner this is over, the better for all of us.

It's almost one in the afternoon. We're all standing around the kitchen unsure how to proceed after the lecture.

"Does anyone want nachos with me?" Liam asks as he heads to the fridge.

Food. Lunch. I wonder why I never get interrupted with thoughts of eating. In the past I have gone almost 36 hours without eating. I get so wrapped up in my work that I don't even think about food. Sleep has always won out over hunger. But suddenly I'm starving.

Liam makes his nachos, and Grace and Sofie pull some late greens from the garden. Dad is frying up some cold cuts and cheese to put on a bulky roll. My standby is cereal. Today I grab our biggest mixing bowl and fill it with three-quarters of a box of Special K. I finish the milk and head to the sink to rinse out the plastic container. As I turn the water on, I notice that Dad is staring at my bowl.

"Was that the last of the milk?" he asks without looking at me.

"I think so. I didn't see another one in the fridge," I say, unsure of why there is so much drama around finishing the milk.

All the motion in the kitchen has stopped and everyone is looking at my bowl. Suddenly I realize what they all seem to have processed already. This is the last milk we will have for a long time. Even if the power stays on, the milk left in the stores will expire today or tomorrow. The last time it was stocked was probably over a week ago. We don't have a cow or even know how to care for or milk a cow.

It's bigger than milk. Stuff is running out and the people that make and deliver that stuff are not around to replace it. Today it was milk, but soon it will be meats, fruits and vegetables. Maybe Dad's sit-tight policy is not as successful as he thought it would be.

"You better eat every drop of that cereal, young man." My father says in an angry voice.

Why is he mad at me? Somebody had to use the last of it. He never warned me to save milk for someone else. What was I supposed to do, let it go bad in our fridge?

"Enjoy the last milk on the planet son," he says with a smile.

I don't get why pretending to be mad at me is funny for him. Maybe he was mad but realized halfway through that he had no right to be. Then he tried to turn it into a joke so we couldn't see how reactive he really is? I don't get it, but it seems like his lame humor has snapped everyone back to their food.

"I think we should keep track of the time since most of the population died. I have been referring to Sunday as the day of the apocalypse and the days since as Post-Apocalypse Day x. That makes today Post-Apocalypse Day three, which I abbreviate to PAD-3." I offer this, trying to take advantage of the relaxed but quiet period.

I'm very proud of my new system. It is clear and simple. You can always work your way back to the beginning and there is no ambiguity from repeating the names of days.

"You mean like change the names on the calendar?" Liam asks, a confused look on his face.

"Well, we don't need to even keep a calendar. For example we are leaving on PAD-5. There is no confusion about when that is. It's two days from today. I spoke to Mom on PAD-2, which was one day ago. No confusion about this Friday or next Friday, yesterday or last Tuesday. My new system is very clean." My pride is showing in my voice.

"I get it. Kind of makes sense." Sofie is on board. Her smile gives me a confidence and warmth I'm not familiar with.

"I'm surprised, Seamus." Dad does not seem open to my idea. "The calendar is a measurement tool that has been in development for over two thousand years. Leap year is a little bit of a kludge and I can agree to get rid of daylight saving time, but on the whole, the current calendar is a system worth keeping."

I'm impressed and embarrassed at the same time. He's right, and he made his point the same way I would have made mine: Concise, accurate and with complete disregard for the other person's feelings.

"We should mark the day, though." Grace is trying to help me save face. "I think Seamus is right, last Sunday, October 5, 2014, should be remembered as the day of the apocalypse."

Nods all around. No new calendar, but we have the first post-apocalyptic holiday recorded.

"Change of plans," Dad says as he cleans up his empty

lunch plate. "Seamus, I need you to look at the connection to the power grid at the gas station. I want you to understand how to connect your power pack or some other generator to get the pumps working. When the power plants eventually stop working, having access to gas will make our lives much easier."

Is he punishing me for not telling him where I was going? If I were an adult, there would be no punishment. Maybe I should tell him that if he wants us to act like adults he has to treat us like adults even when we screw up.

"Liam, I need you and Grace to start organizing our stuff. Lay things out in the dining room in order of priority. Water, food, sleeping bags, and so on. There are five of us, and I want the food and water to last five days if it has to." Dad is moving on. I hope that he doesn't become irrational and leave out my lab to prove a point. That would be ridiculous.

"Sofie, I'm sorry, but I need you to hang out at the gas station with Seamus. I just don't want any of you split up and left on your own. Maybe you can take notes for Seamus or find a paper atlas." He's really rolling now.

This definitely does not feel like punishment. A couple of hours alone with Sofie feels like a dream come true.

"No problem, Paddrick. I'll help any way I can." Sofie is not acting like an adult. She is an adult. How is it that she knows how to be an adult? What could I possibly learn in a year that will help me to behave more like an adult? This is the social aspect of life Dad is always talking to me about. I have always found these things immeasurable, un-teachable and utterly frustrating.

"Where are you going, Daddy?" Grace asks. I've never been able to tell why she slips into her little-girl mode. I don't think Dad likes it but he rarely speaks a harsh word to Grace, so he would never say so.

"I'm going to get a new car." He is smiling from ear to ear. Dad really likes cars. It's not quite a love thing, but he has this thing about how many different cars he has driven. Some days it seems as if he likes the 8-year old mini van as much as the new Porsche Cayenne.

"What kind?" Liam asks, never hearing a conversation he couldn't jump in the middle of.

"I'm thinking Cadillac. I want the biggest, fanciest SUV they have. We are going cross-country in style!" Dad is still smiling.

I realize that he is also looking for a tank. The Cadillac SUV is the closest thing to a luxury armored personnel carrier you can get. If we are all going to work and survive as a team, Dad has to stop keeping details from us. He thinks he and Mom are great at the parenting trick of distracting us with the bright shiny aspect of the awful truth. Fact is that Grace and Liam may still fall for it, but I don't, and I doubt that Sofie does either.

"That'll be one hell of a battle wagon," Sofie says, securing her place in the adult camp by swearing and calling Dad out on his real motive.

We talk about cars as we finish our food, then Grace and Sofie clean up the kitchen while I grab my iPad and stylus.

"Seamus, you and Sofie can take the Cayenne to the gas station. Drive carefully, though; there is a lot of power in that car and you are not used to it." Dad is trying to get things rolling. I can tell he's worried about getting home before dark. This fear of the darkness has me concerned. I hope his mind isn't slipping under the stress.

"No problem. We shouldn't be there long. I've spent quite a bit of time studying and modifying our electric panel. I don't see why theirs would be much different." I am on the razor edge between confidence and arrogance. I'm 16 and I am about to get into a Porsche Cayenne with a beautiful girl, drive up the street and assess an electric panel. If this isn't my wheelhouse, I don't have one.

"Do. Not. Touch. Anything." Dad has his eyes fixed on me. He articulates and emphasizes each word for effect. For a second I think there is a problem in the house, but then I realize he is referring to the gas station. I'm not really sure what he's talking about. When it comes to electricity and power, I know what I am doing. He shouldn't be giving me orders.

"Okay Dad." Oops, that was too dismissive. I hold my breath waiting for the lecture to begin, but it doesn't. He's looking at me but says nothing. Maybe he can see in my face that I know I was wrong. This is how he should have been punishing me for years. Lectures are easily forgotten; this feeling of stewing in my wrongness will last.

There is a flurry of action and Dad is out the door. Grace and Liam have an iPad and are making an inventory of essentials. I hope they have it in a spreadsheet so it can be easily reordered if they make a mistake. I'm ready to explain to them the right way to go about their assignment when Sofie puts her arm around me.

"Come on, genius. Let's go to the gas station."

Driving has never held much allure for me. But behind the wheel of the Porsche I can see what it is Dad loves about cars. The balance, the power, the control. It is a piece of engineering marvel. If only it didn't use the antiquated internal combustion engine. Sofie really should take this for a spin. This thought makes me realize how little we know about her. Her family could have been rich or poor. She may have brothers and sisters, aunts and uncles. I've never spoken to her about these things. Is this what she and Grace have been talking about since they met?

I'm ready to ask her about her family, but we just arrived at the gas station. The fifteen-minute walk is about a four-minute drive. This shouldn't take long, but maybe I'll drag it out so I have more time with Sofie.

I guess the front door is the best place to start. For some reason, it surprises me that it is unlocked. I can feel Sofie's tension as we go through the door and into the small office. Did she sense the fear in me or is there something else that has her on high alert? Suddenly I want to make quick work of this assignment. I have three days in a car to get to know Sofie.

"Where to?" Sofie whispers.

I have no idea where the power comes into the gas station. The quiet engulfs us and there is an uneasiness that permeates the room. I feel exposed and vulnerable. I was hoping to be seen as brave but self-deprecating will have to do.

"Back outside. I don't even know where the power comes into the building," I say, a little too loud and with a broad smile.

I spin around and head out the door. I feel Sofie's hands on my back and a light push.

"You dork! I was so scared. Don't ever do that to me again," she says, but she's laughing a little. She knows I didn't do anything.

I follow the power lines into the building. Power to the pumps must run underground from the building, because I don't see any visible connection.

Back inside, I find the breaker panel easily in one of the garage bays. Sofie is rooting around the office. There was a rack for paper maps in plain sight, but it was empty. The idea of a physical atlas feels antiquated, like something circa Christopher Columbus.

The panel has a pair of fifty-amp fuses labeled "Pump Sub." I realize this may take more time than I thought. Hopefully the pump sub is in the office?

In the office, Sofie is bent over the bottom drawer of a filing cabinet. I have to squeeze by her to get to what looks like the panel for the pumps. Touching her sends a shiver up my spine. I know that it's hormones and adrenaline rushing through my veins, but the warmth feels good, and confusing. I have to pause and collect my thoughts.

Does she have any idea how she makes me feel? Maybe this is how every guy she has ever met acts so it seems totally normal. Or maybe I'm weird and I frighten her.

I open the little door and find keys on hangers. Some are labeled with numbers, others with letters. Nothing useful. And I'm still distracted with feelings and self-made drugs. So I slam the door and growl.

"Can I ask you something?" Sofie is looking up at me with a puzzled look. "Why is anger your first reaction to everything?"

It's not, though. My first reaction to this question is embarrassment. Anger is not an emotion I have ever associated with myself. Frustrated and annoyed sure, but never angered. Is this how other people have always seen me? The angry nerd?

"Back home, I worked in a coffee shop." Sofie is staring at nothing, remembering a past that she shares only with herself. "The smartest man in our town, maybe even the whole world, used to sit in a booth for hours on end. People from all over would come in and see him. There were never introductions, they just sat down across from him and he would ask, 'How are you? What's going on?' Some people were short and to the point; others told long stories that just ended with no real question being asked."

I want to tell her that people asking you questions does not make you smart, it makes them dumb. But it seems like she wants to get this off her chest so I sit quietly.

"He never had answers for them. He would just ask them questions. Some would get up and run out after a few questions, others sat quietly and enjoyed coffee," she says. She is now smiling and I think her story is over.

I don't see the point. How does any of this relate to me, or show me that this guy was smart. "So what made him so smart?" I ask with a contorted face.

"That right there. Embracing questions, enjoying what he didn't know. Curiosity." She's back to the filing drawer and going through papers. I've got to get on with my project, I'll think about her "lesson" later. One thing's for sure, though: I'm going to work on not growling at people.

Maybe her story and Dad's story about the hockey guy go together. I have more time than I think and it's okay to not know the answer, learn from the questions. Like where is the panel for the pump sub? It should be obvious, right out in the open.

Then I realize that I live in a small town in New Hampshire. They have not changed the pumps or electrical configuration at this gas station in forty years. So I crawl under the counter and head towards the cash register. There on the wall of the cabinet is a breaker panel with a piece of masking tape across the front. Faintly written in what might be crayon is "Pumps." I grab the handle and open the door, expecting to find two circuit breakers, one for each pump. But there are eight and they are not labeled.

I start following wires. There is white-and-black shielded electrical wire, and they seem to be bundled with blue Cat5. It's easy enough to get out of the breaker panel, but I lose the line I'm tracing quickly. This is spaghetti. They must have updated the pump system more recently than I had expected. Except they seem to have done so with leftover wire and scraps from other projects.

Finding where the power comes into the sub is my priority. The trunk line is grey and easily identified, but it goes through a device I have never seen before. It's almost like an emergency shut-off, but it appears to be homemade.

It's been more than an hour and I completely forgot about Sofie. Where is she? I hope she wasn't talking to me. The panel and wires had me so wrapped up I was deaf to anything else. Now I'm worried. She could have been taken or fallen and injured. I need to find her and make sure she's safe. Not only have I not made progress with the pumps, I've lost Sofie.

I burst out of the office door, ready to yell her name, when something catches the corner of my eye. I spin to my right and assume the closest thing to a fighting stance that I can imagine. There's Sofie, sitting on the beat-up old chair in front of the garage. She's got the atlas on her lap and she looks over at me smiling. "Figure it out, Exxon?"

"No, I didn't. You can't just leave without telling me," I say. We cannot afford to be careless and flighty if we want to survive. I'm angry but relieved.

"I didn't leave, I just came outside." She's smiling, and beautiful.

I want to scream at her. Instead I decide to turn my emotions loose on the office.

"Well there's one thing I want to try before we leave." I'm not conversational, just stating a fact, as I turn to go back into the building.

"Okay, but remember that your Dad said not to touch anything!" She's yelling after me as if I'm miles away. How can she not tell that I'm angry with her? Or does she know I'm angry and she just doesn't care?

Inside the gas station, I knock the computer and all the other junk off the counter. I'm not being quiet or delicate. This is a bonus of post-apocalyptic life, efficiency. After the crap is cleared, I pull up on the laminate countertop itself. Sports were never my forte so I'm not strong, but the top doesn't even seem to be fastened to the cabinets. It comes off easily. I should have done this an hour ago.

With the area of interest more exposed to light, I should be able to work faster. I grab a screwdriver and a pair of pliers. My anger has come down a level, but I am working quickly and efficiently.

At the pump sub-panel, I go right to work on the top of the box. I can't imagine what this unit does; I have never seen one before. The four screws are removed and I am not very careful pulling the cover off; what I'm interested in is inside. The cover snags on something, but I pull a little more firmly and it comes right off.

The words "Tamper Proof 9000" are stenciled above a display that reads "LOCKED," and I see a place for a wire to be inserted or a pin reset button. There are two electrical wires and a blue Cat5 wire coming out of the bottom of the unit, but no other information. This isn't a real product; it's some hack from the owner/manager who was too cheap to pay for a real solution.

I don't understand this setup. As I look around the office for clues, I remember the cover. I'm starting to piece things together. There's a wire attached to the cover. I take the stripped end of the wire and feed it into the unit where it seems to be an obvious fit. I expect the screen to change to "UNLOCK," but it doesn't. Uh-oh.

Sofie walks through the door with a smirk. "You're supposed to be inspecting an electric panel, not redecorating."

She's laughing a little. I bet she knows she drove me to destroy the office. Even though it was the best way to work efficiently, I do not like it when emotion takes over. It may be funny to her, but not to me.

The bell indicating a new customer has arrived dings and it seems so loud it could shatter the windows. Sofie screams and jumps four feet across the room and right into my arms. I've inhaled so deeply that I'm worried that all the air in the tiny office is gone, and it feels like I'm suffocating.

I look out the window and see Dad climbing out of a Cadillac Escalade with an ear-to-ear grin. I didn't even realize how much tension there was. We have been doing such a good job of faking confidence that I forgot there was a gnawing fear in my subconscious, and apparently I'm not alone. "It's okay, just my dad coming for gas," I say quietly into Sofie's ear. Her hair smells so good. Feeling her body pressed so close to mine is beyond words.

Dad is through the door, "Okay, break it up you two." He must know he scared us both because he is not teasing or pretending to be upset. He gives Sofie a minute to let go of me before he continues. "I see you did some redecorating. I would like a million dollars on pump one, please." The idea of free gas has my father almost giddy.

"I don't think it's going to work Dad." I'm working on a story that doesn't make me look bad but I don't have it yet.

"What happened?" Dad has lost the giddiness. "Did you fill the Cayenne when you got here?"

Hmmm, understanding a baseline before you begin tampering with something makes sense. I know this, but these damn hormones are not helping.

"No. I found this thing called the 'Tamper Proof 9000,' and it reads 'LOCKED.' It's at the top of the pump sub panel and I think it controls the pumps." So far, I haven't lied.

"Was the office torn apart when you got here?" Dad may be ahead of me on figuring this one out.

"No, I did that trying to figure out these pumps," I offer, still not sure what I am going to say about this. I can see no reason why the pumps would not have worked when we got here, but I don't know for sure. What I do know for sure is that they don't work now. Do I confess to my Dad that I broke them and didn't follow his direction not to touch anything, or do I let this go as a mystery and hope he doesn't push?

Dad's thinking. And he is mad, I can tell by his face and the fact that he isn't saying anything. He looks around the office but doesn't move. I probably look guilty, if that helps him make up his mind.

"Okay, it's almost dark and we need to get moving. Time for Plan B." Dad is on his way out the door. I have never been a fan of "Plan B." If you have time to spend making a "Plan B," it means you should have spent more time on Plan A to ensure that it would work. I usually quit if I find out that Plan A doesn't work. Dad doesn't have the option of quitting, and neither do I.

I follow Dad out to the Cadillac as he is getting in the driver's seat. "Go back inside and look for a pump. Also see if there is anything to indicate what type of fuel the underground tanks hold. Even though this ride was free, I don't want to put diesel in and ruin it. That would be a hassle."

I can't tell if he's mad or just motivated. Sofie is standing in the parking lot in some sort of limbo.

Then she speaks: "Where are you going?"

"I'm going to the garage to get a pump and some hose," he says, just before pulling out.

CHAPTER 10

As I lie in bed, I'm recapping how yesterday ended. Filling the cars with gas turned out to be pretty easy. If we had gone with the plan of pumping it directly out of the ground tanks in the first place, it would have been quicker and far less stressful. But if we have to bring the pump and hoses for every fill-up they will take up space in the Cadillac. That space could have been used for my lab equipment.

Sofie went home ahead of us and when we arrived she and Grace were working on dinner. I'm glad Gracie likes to cook, and she is good at it. We basically had a feast; steaks, chicken, shrimp and grilled vegetables. Whatever we wanted to eat and as much as we wanted. The freezer was emptied and there was no anxiety about waste. If we didn't eat it, we couldn't have used it anyway.

Liam and Dad washed the dishes and Dad cleaned up around the kitchen. I guess some of his habits are hard to break. Grace, Sofie and I acted like it was Thanksgiving and headed to the family room and put on a movie. We were semi-catatonic when Dad and Liam came in, but then everyone was asleep within minutes.

Not getting the pumps to work is still gnawing at me, probably why I'm awake at 5:20 in the morning. I know I have only hurt myself. Another approach to the problem isn't clear to me though. Sure, I didn't have to tear apart the office, but that really had no effect on the pumps. I had to take that cover off to know what was underneath. I don't really consider it "touching" the system when I just remove a cosmetic component to inspect inner workings. How could I have known it wasn't just cosmetic?

I doubt that Dad thinks I really did anything either. While I was standing with the pump filling the Cadillac, he inspected the "Tamper Proof 9000." All he said when he came back out is, "That's a weird setup. Did the cover come off easy?" Fortunately the truth is that it did come off easy. My "Yup" was true and natural, so we left it at that. The rest of the time filling the gas tank was spent with speculation about other gas stations, particularly those along the highway, and their use of anti-tampering devices. A garden hose and a sump pump take a lot longer to fill a tank than the regular gas pump.

This frustration is getting me nowhere. I might as well get up and work on packing the lab. Dad has given me two long Thule roof carriers. I know it is generous and accommodating, but it's not nearly enough space for the things I want to bring.

While my father tells people I have an eidetic memory, the truth is I don't. Dad does not know the definition of the term eidetic. I have a high IQ, some innate memory skills, and have developed tools to help me. I rely on a database when the volume of information is high. My lab inventory database is killer. Several terabytes of data stored in the cloud with a mirror on a local server in the corner. Not only do I have every piece of equipment inventoried, I also have all the experiments and tests inventoried. At any time I can see what I am using a given piece of equipment for, the types of interconnects needed, and the time left until the equipment will be available for other experiments.

Standing in my lab, I am torn. Do I pack based on experiment or equipment value?

I think equipment. I survey my space looking at the size of individual items. If there is something that's too big, I can easily rule it out and move on. But there is nothing that can't be broken down small enough to fit in the space I have allotted in the Thule's. Small, tight and efficient has been the priority for my reactor, and it has held true for my development equipment, too. I wonder if I should add a physical dimension field to the equipment database? It seems weird that I don't already have that. I guess physical space restraints have never been a part of my life.

I decide to evaluate based on processor code. A great deal of my work has taken advantage of existing microprocessors. I find used ones online and buy them cheap or I get them free from local electronic recycling days. The result is spaghetti code. Some of the programming interfaces are older and not intuitive. When the internet goes down for good, I may not be able to get back to the information I need to properly modify syntax.

I run a report based on coding language and then sort the results into an ordered list. This may turn out to be a valuable exercise. I see that there are a few processors I have replacements for and others that I am no longer using.

Now that I have a plan of attack, I can start powering things down. In eight years, I have never powered down my entire lab at the same time. I see another shortcoming in my documentation. No shutdown procedure. I have no advanced experiments running, but still I need to pause before I shut down each piece of equipment. If it is controlling another device or aggregating data from somewhere, I need to power down the remote before I power down the control. Nothing catastrophic will occur if I don't, but I hate parsing through error logs that I have created.

I'm not sure why I didn't know it would take this long. I could really use an assistant. But I could never work with anyone if they weren't almost as smart as me. Having a lab partner at school was like high comedy. I would be sorting the results of the experiment, thinking of derivatives of the data and criticizing the teacher while my partner was reading the first sentence. It wasn't because I did the experiment quickly either. It was because I could tell what answer they wanted before the experiment started. It was never about learning; it was always about getting the answer right.

"Seamus, do you want breakfast?" Liam is yelling down the stairs. Volume control was never his strength.

Oddly, I'm at a perfect time for a break. It still annoys me that Liam is the one interrupting me. "Yeah, I'll be up in a minute," I answer back quietly, trying to make the point that the yelling is unnecessary.

Upstairs, Dad has waffles, apples with cinnamon, bacon, eggs, sausages, and toast cooked. No cereal; I had the last of the milk. Otherwise the feast mentality has continued to breakfast. Sofie is trying to help but Dad won't let her.

"You're a guest in our house. You don't serve breakfast," he tells her as he swats at her hand with a spatula.

"But I grew up in a coffee shop, breakfast is totally my thing!" she protests.

Grace is busy working on a breakfast soundtrack. She's calling out songs that Liam and Sofie are saying yes or no to. Then she moves it into a playlist and the beat goes on. And that's Gracie, trying to put on a happy face for everything and everyone. I wonder if she can really be as oblivious as she acts sometimes or if it's calculated because she knows it's comforting for the rest of us.

"I think Seamus could still learn a thing or two about domestic chores," Dad says, looking over at me. It's like he waited until I sat down.

"I don't see why anyone has to be a server, can't we just fend for ourselves?" I've sucked the fun right out of the room. This is the problem with being myself. I'm a total downer. Just because I was able to take a break from the lab doesn't mean I shut my brain off and switched to party mode.

"Lighten up, Seamus, we're just having fun." It's Liam's turn to say it. If there were a word cloud for my life, *"Lighten up, Seamus"* would probably be the largest.

"Carrying a plate for someone you like is not work." Sofie has grabbed two plates of food and is heading to the table.

Wow, she likes me. I can't believe I'm having this debate about whether she likes me or like likes me. If it's "like" like's me, are we ready to tell everyone else? Seven billion people died in the last week; now might not be an appropriate time to start or announce a relationship. Or maybe she likes me in the way she likes an old sweatshirt—something nice and good to have around, but no real loss if it disappears.

"Oooh, Sofie likes Seamus," Liam says in his best schoolyard taunting voice.

"Liam, I like all of you." Sofie shows no sign of being embarrassed that would lead me to think that there was some truth to Liam's teasing. "In fact, I'm conflicted about how happy and comfortable I am here with you. Everyone I have ever known is dead. Fresh food is becoming scarce and we are about to leave on a potentially dangerous trip. But for some reason I can't stop dancing to Grace's soundtrack and smiling every time I see one of you walk into the room."

"Well, we're sorry about the circumstances, but we are all glad to have you around. You're an impressive young woman and I am happy we can call you a friend." Dad thinks he's accepting an award. He's walked to the table with two more plates of food. Grace turns from the computer and sits at her place where Dad has put the second plate. Liam is the odd man out, but this is okay, he never sits down for long anyway. He's got a plate and continually moves about the kitchen while he picks at the food.

"Dad, breakfast is great as usual. Thanks for making the eggs the way I like them!" Grace loves her "pleases" and "thank you's." She almost seems fake with her effervescent gratitude, but it is completely genuine.

"Yeah, thanks for breakfast Dad," I add through a mouthful of waffles. I'm still kind of full from last night's feast and rarely do I actually eat two meals in a row, but somehow sitting here feels right.

When I'm done chewing, I take a moment to gear myself up. I need to ask for help, but this is hard for me. I want it to be Sofie that helps, for a number of reasons, not the least of which is her sure hands. I'm worried that it will look like I am trying to manufacture alone time with her. I can't say that's the furthest thing from my mind, but it is not the absolute top right now.

"Seamus, do you need any help in your lab?" Sofie is looking at me but I can't tell if her eyes are hopeful or just open. "I packed my things a few days ago and it seems like Grace, Liam and your Dad have a method of working together on packing." She shovels a scoop of scrambled eggs into her mouth.

"That would be really helpful." I brace myself for the teasing from Liam or Dad. "Thank you."

"Well, finish eating and get to work. It's already after ten. I don't mind getting done early, but I don't want to be up all night." Dad is on edge.

We've packed up for vacations plenty of times before, but this is different. If we forget something, we aren't coming back to get it. We all know that food and water are the priority, but if we are going to start over we need to bring some of the little things that help define who we are.

"If we took an RV, that would be cool. We could cook and walk around while Dad drives." Liam chimes in with a classic non sequitur. His thinking is so non-linear it's scary. I cannot even imagine how he got from packing and getting done early to taking an RV. How do other people have so much patience with him? I find him to be totally insane.

"You know, I thought about that," Dad replies. "There are a few reasons that make an RV impractical. The first of which is speed. I drove an RV to Canada once, and it did not feel safe above 55 miles an hour. I want to go much faster than that. The second is gas mileage. The Escalade isn't great, but we should not have to stop more than four or five times to fill up."

Something else comes to my mind; we should be assuming that we are not alone, and, if we are alone, the vigilance won't hurt. If we're not alone, then planning and some luck may be our only assets. An RV is plenty safe while driving, but defending an RV from attackers or doing evasive maneuvers would be tricky. I think we are going to wind up camping on the top floor of hotels. This is an aspect of the apocalypse that doesn't seem to have dawned on my siblings quite yet.

I've finished my meal and see a chance to work on those domestic skills, so I clear the others' plates and quickly wash up the pans. My mind is still churning on the possibility of dark and scary survivors, but by the time the dishes are done I seem to have washed those thoughts away. It's just easier to keep moving that way.

Dad has Grace and Liam carrying things out to the driveway. He likes to lay the stuff out near the car before he puts things in. This way he can arrange and rearrange for hours until he gets it the way he wants it.

Sofie and I head down to the lab and set to work. There are a few more devices to power down, but she can start carrying things out to the car. I have them lined up on a workbench in order of importance.

"If you can carry some things out to the car it would be great. Just grab stuff from the front of that lineup on the bench. You can leave them on the grass near the car. I'm not sure if Dad wants to put them in the overheads or if he expects me to."

And she's off. It's nice not to play twenty questions with someone so they can help me. Once I get these last things powered down, I can start carrying things out, too. This may not take as long as I thought.

"Your dad said it was okay to load things in the overheads, so I did. As you look at the front of the car, I started with the left overhead and put the first item at the back." Sofie was only halfway down the stairs before she started talking. I love the detail and precision. If this were Liam, he would have split the things he brought up between both carriers and put them in the middle. Sofie can tell that they were lined up for a reason and there is some value to the order. I wonder if this is how she thinks too, or if the things that Grace has told her about me have her trying to act a certain way.

"Thank you, that's really helpful." I'm grinning widely. I'm happy that she's here, happy that it's going well.

"Can I ask you what it is that you work on so hard in this lab of yours?" She's leaning on the bench and surveying my basement lair.

"I'm developing a loss-less power reactor that creates a huge amount of energy from a very small amount of catalyst." No one has ever really asked me this directly before, so my answer is not well rehearsed.

"How did you learn about all this stuff? Grace says you're like some kind of physics genius but she doesn't know how you got so smart." My new, if temporary, assistant is holding a box of circuit boards and looking at me intently.

"Well, I'm not sure how I got smart. Genetics is the best guess. As for how I learned everything, the Internet is amazing. When I was eight, I asked my dad about a nuclear reactor. He couldn't answer my questions, so we searched online. The pictures of atoms with the nucleus, protons, electrons and neutrons were all so clear to me. Everything made sense except that I saw something missing. Reading and research lead me to dark energy and I thought it was pretty obvious how it fit. The rest has just been building blocks to get where I wanted to go."

I am secretly excited that she talked to Grace about me.

"And do you think you will ever be able to do it?" Sofie is trying not to sound skeptical, but failing.

"Actually, I finalized the design last week. I know it will work, I just need a few more days to put the design into implementation." I'm very proud of myself. She has no idea of the breakthrough she will be witnessing in the coming weeks.

"Cool. I look forward to seeing this invention of yours working." With that, she has another armful of equipment and is headed up the stairs.

The last experiments are powered down and I have a chance to carry at least half of my things up to the car. Everything fits well in the overheads with a little bit of space remaining for any last-second things. It's almost three and I think we'll be done packing early.

Tomorrow we leave New Hampshire, probably forever.

CHAPTER 11

I'm seething. I don't know why I am so mad, but I am, and everyone can tell. I'm trying to pass it off as having to get out of bed at 5 a.m., but we all got up at the same time. It's just the front seat; it doesn't mean anything. But why is Sofie there? If it were Grace, would I be this mad? Probably not, because that would mean Sofie would be sitting in the back with me. If it were Liam, forget about it; I would be bouncing off the walls in rage.

Mom always says she loves to ride in the back. It makes her feel like a celebrity. Dad wants a private jet, but Mom wants a driver, even if it's for our beat-up minivan. They go well together with their caviar dreams. Right now, I feel like a child. It seems like Dad has the car segregated, just like when he and Mom take us places. Grown-ups are in front, kids in back.

We are living up to the term "kids," too. There are three DVD screens and we have been bickering for an hour about what to watch and on which screens. I wouldn't mind watching what they want to watch, but I'm being difficult just to be difficult. I really need to rein it in. Deep breaths.

"You know what? I'm sorry for being difficult. Go ahead and watch whatever." I may have given Dad a heart attack with my honesty. Grace and Liam don't know what to do with me. They may start fighting just to maintain a small shred of normalcy.

"It's just that I feel weird that we left in kind of a rush and didn't get to say goodbye to our stuff." I'm staring out the window as I say words I haven't thought about but somehow know are true.

"Seamus, it's not like you didn't know we were leaving. We spent yesterday packing and we've been talking about it for a few days. I thought you had plenty of time to say goodbye." Dad is defensive and I can tell he feels bad that I am hurting.

"It came pretty fast for me, too." Grace is trying to hold back the tears. "We spent most of our lives in that house. Sure, we've been places, but we always got to go home. And that felt good."

"I just wanna see Mom." Liam is a people person. He likes people but he *loves* his family, and I think that not having Mom around has been killing him. This is a rare occasion when he has nothing else to say and stares blankly out the window.

"I know what you mean, buddy, I can't wait to get to California either." Dad has a forced smile but you can almost feel how badly he misses Mom.

"All I can think about is the adventure. This is interesting to be able to see these different parts of the country. You don't get this experience when you fly over in an airplane." Sofie is quiet and working hard to keep her eyes and mind on the scenery whizzing past.

"Sofie, is that Canada over there?" Grace is trying to shift the topic, but this is not the right direction. Our family is all together and sad about leaving our house and anxious about meeting up with Mom. Sofie has nothing left. She left her house days ago and everyone in her family is dead.

"I'm angry because I didn't get to sit in the front seat." I'm not sure where this is going or how it will help. It seems like no one else can figure out what to say either. "Isn't that ridiculous?" I continue. "I know there is no reason for it to matter and it's a silly thing to care about, but for some reason I do."

By now I don't even want to sit in the front seat. I've gotten over my jealousy and feel like calmly sitting in the back helps me be more mature. "Or I did."

"I'm sorry for forcing a seating arrangement. I just thought that if we did things like we always have, with you three in the back, it would be a little more normal." It's Dad's turn to kind of stare blankly out the window. "And I gotta say that with your bickering and arguing it has felt like every other road trip to me."

"Sorry, Dad." Grace is half-hearted with her apology. She's not sure if she is supposed to feel bad about fighting or if it is a good thing to make this feel like every other road trip. Liam is just sitting in silence and has nothing to add.

We ride in limbo like this for a long time. I'm not sure what the others are thinking, but I am debating the value of efforts to make things feel like they used to. Life will never be the same. Pretending like nothing has changed will not help us survive. Dad may have already shifted his brain, but the rest of us need to get there. Our new cares are food, water and shelter. But it's hard to adopt that mindset while I sit here in the plush leather seats of a stolen Cadillac Escalade.

"Dad, where are we?" Of course it's Liam who breaks the silence.

"We're on I-84 in Connecticut. New York is next." Dad is so proud of his knowledge of the U.S. interstate system and how it flows through states across the country.

"Is Connecticut part of New England?" Liam is thinking about geography, which I guess make sense on a road trip.

"Yes." Dad does not elaborate or provide insightful commentary. Sometimes we can get him talking about random things and he'll tell us stories that mix fact, fiction and opinion. It can be really entertaining, but he doesn't seem in the mood for it now.

"How is our average speed?" I ask, self-noting my interest in measurable facts.

"Not bad, we're at about one hundred. Considering the

time we spent slogging through those back roads to get to the highway, we're making good time." Dad is proud of the car's ability to record data. He can be simple at times.

"Where do you think we are going to stop tonight?" Sofie is coming out of her funk.

"I would love to push through to Indiana, at the very least." Dad has a plan but I know he is notorious for overestimating time and distance. "We'll need to stop for gas soon. That will likely dictate how far we are able to get before nightfall."

"Are you worried that we won't be able to find gas?" Liam asks.

"No, Liam. Gas didn't disappear. I just don't know how easy it will be for us to get it out of the tank and into the car." Dad is frustrated, but I don't think it's just with Liam's question.

Then I see it. Up ahead there is black smoke rising in the sky. It looks like it is coming up directly from the highway. I can't tell how far away it is. While the possibilities are not endless, I can't even guess at what is causing the smoke. Things don't just blow up or catch on fire. There hasn't been a lightning storm, so I know that it's not a fire sparked by "natural causes."

A quick glance at the navigation screen shows that we are coming up to a river. What if there are a lot of survivors and they have joined together on the other side of that river and won't let anyone across? What if humankind is making its last stand in Newburgh, New York?

The Escalade is slowing down, but I don't see anything. "Seamus, could you and Liam get a couple of the rifles loaded and at the ready?" Dad is on high alert and his head is on a swivel. I see him move the sidearm from the center console into his waistband. Since we have had the guns he has been saying, "never John Wayne it, weapons needed to be stored and secured properly." I guess the rules still don't apply for him.

"Dad, do you really think that there are a bunch of

survivors holed up in Newburgh trying to keep other people from crossing the river?" I don't know Newburgh from anything, but it seems like a pretty random place to me.

"Seamus, West Point is just down the river from here. We are coming to the closest major bridge across the Hudson River. If there are any remnants of the U.S. government fighting to protect what they consider an uninfected population, I think that West Point would be a pretty logical place to be. They could effectively shut down and defend this bridge with a handful of people." Dad was never in the military, but I know I never thought of tactics like this.

My amazement at how Dad can think of a defensive strategy for the remaining vestiges of humankind must be similar to how he feels when I talk about my reactor. They may be baby steps, but I'm understanding more and more why he has always told me that I can't know everything. It doesn't matter how smart you are, if you are not exposed to certain basic things, you can't know anything about them.

We're down to 65 miles per hour and it feels like we are crawling. In the car there is silence, as if we may hear something that will tip us off to impending danger. Liam and I are holding loaded rifles in the third row. Grace is defenseless in the middle row and Sofie is staring intently out the front window.

The bridge across the Hudson River is now visible. There are no clear signs of danger. No warning signs to turn back, no bombed-out cars, and no military vehicles blocking the road. There is one road crossing over the highway and then we have a straight shot to the bridge.

As we approach the road going over the highway, the wreck becomes clear. A black charred automobile is up against the bridge abutment in the center median. There are no flames or people around, just black smoke slowly rising up. It's impossible to tell what type of vehicle it was or when this happened. It's recent, but not new. There are no survivors and stopping would be pointless.

"Probably the tires still burning that's causing all that

smoke." Dad sounds exhausted all of the sudden. "I hate to say it, but I'm glad that's all it is."

We continue on over the bridge at 65 mph. We're back to silence, but it is very different from the silence we had while we approached the bridge. Someone died in that car wreck. Were they running from something? Were they running *to* something? Why do we seem to be so lucky when all these other people are unlucky? Not even unlucky, *dying*.

Eventually the Escalade is back up to 110 miles per hour. I'm not sure what everyone else is thinking about, but I realize that I kind of hoped that there were a bunch of survivors defending the bridge. It feels like a better fate than being the only humans left on Earth.

The next hour passes in silence. In the back, we lose ourselves in a movie. Upfront, Sofie is intermittently nodding off to sleep and watching the scenery. I can't even imagine what Dad is thinking about, but he is driving and working to keep the average speed above 100.

A gas pit stop somewhere in Pennsylvania is surprisingly uneventful. We pull up to the pumps and Dad fills her up. "While we have electricity, should we pay cash for gas?" Dad says loud enough to get through the car windows. For a second I expect him to walk to the cashier booth and leave money. I can already hear him saying, "It's the right thing to do," but he doesn't. He hangs up the pump, hops into the Escalade, and we are off. I wonder if he had this kind of moral dilemma when he obtained the Escalade in the first place.

As we pull out of the rest area Dad tosses his phone back to me. "Seamus, open up Trulia and find the most expensive home in Akron, Ohio." Trulia is how Mom and Dad voyeuristically watch the real estate market. I'm not sure why he wants to look at a home in Ohio, though, and it seems like kind of a non sequitur.

"Okay, I'll bite," says Sofie from the front seat. "Why are you interested in Ohio real estate?"

"Are we going to stay in Ohio for a few days?" asks Liam from the back seat. I seriously wish he would think before he speaks. That is the dumbest thing he could have said.

Dad has learned to not even answer the dumbest of questions from him. "I'm looking for a place to spend the night," he says evenly.

"Why not just go to a hotel and crash there?" This is the quickest Sofie has spoken since we met her. It's not a bad question, but she usually waits to see how things play out before she says anything.

"In my mind, 'hotel' equals 'complicated.' I don't want to worry about how we program a key or how we find and cook food in an industrial kitchen. It just seems like there is a list of things that could make a hotel a hassle." Dad is getting tired.

"Well I suppose the rest of us don't really have a say. But if you ask me, 'hotel' equals 'options.' I have no idea what's going to happen tomorrow and the idea of being in a big safe hotel appeals to me." Sofie is on edge. She used the word "safe," and I am wondering if she worries about paramilitary groups and government agents the way I do.

After a period of silence, Dad lets out a heavy sigh. "Sofie, I understand your perspective and I'm not saying you are wrong. I just want to stay low-key and easy. We find a house, let ourselves in, and we are good for the night. When we get to California, we can move into the fanciest hotel in San Francisco."

It's just dawned on me that low-key and easy is also "incognito." If we lit up the top-floor of a hotel tonight, that would call attention to us. If there is anyone else out there, we would be sitting ducks. I'm not sure this is part of Dad's thought process, but I bet it is. Right now we're playing checkers, and he's playing chess.

"How does six bedrooms, seven and a half baths in 10,000 square feet sound? 30,000 bottle wine cellar, swimming pool and hot tub. All situated on 20 private acres of hills and fields." I'm not usually the one to change the subject. I like to grind things out and make all parties admit the truth. This just seems like a case where moving on will solve a lot of problems.

"A swimming pool!" Grace is sold on this one already.

"How far from the highway is it?" Dad is thinking logistics. It would have been better if he included that parameter when he asked me to look for a place. Fortunately I included that variable on my own.

"Not far," I say with one of my patented sighs.

"How much?" asks Liam. It doesn't matter and the number will be irrelevant to a 15-year-old, but he likes his questions.

"Just over $2 million. I've plugged the address into navigation. It says we are forty minutes away. I bet you can't make it there in twenty," I say as I hand the phone back to Dad.

"You're on," he says, as we accelerate to an almost uncomfortable speed.

CHAPTER 12

It took us twenty-seven minutes to get to the house. Dad was almost reckless on the highway but had no choice other than to slow down on the back roads. Now we have another unforeseen problem: a gate.

Dad hops out of the Escalade and gives the gate a push. It doesn't move. Not even an inch. He examines the gate, presumably for a latch or release of some kind, but has no luck. A last shove on the gate and he is done with it.

"Dad! We can smash through it with the car. No one will care." Liam needs some excitement and his words come out so fast we can barely understand him.

"Sorry, Liam. Not this time." Dad already has the car in drive and we are continuing down the street. "I don't want to risk damaging the car in any way. Transferring our stuff to another vehicle will take too much time."

I see on the navigation screen that the street ends in a cul-de-sac. Dad must be assuming that there is a house or houses around it. As we get closer, his hunch proves correct. There are 4 houses, all big and all beautiful.

"This looks like it was a pretty nice neighborhood," Grace says as we slowly pull up to the circle.

"Technically, it still *is* a pretty nice neighborhood," I say, somewhat wishing I had kept that as inner monologue. "I guess what I mean is that this doesn't look any different now than it did last week before all the people here died. If it was nice then, it's still nice now. If we come back in a few weeks and the grass and plantings are all overgrown, then the past tense would be appropriate."

No one is interested in my semantics. Sometimes Grace will clue me in that correcting people is not the best tactic for making friends, but, given that I corrected her, she doesn't speak up now.

"I suppose that's a debate, whether a neighborhood is defined by the people or the properties. That would have been interesting, emphasis on the past tense there. We don't seem to be in a position where debating relatively trivial things warrants a lot of brainpower. Emphasis on the present tense." Sofie is sticking up for Grace and making a good argument on her behalf.

Dad has parked the car in the second driveway around the cul-de-sac. I'm not sure what he's looking at, but he waits for a few minutes before he turns the engine off and moves his hand to the door.

"Here's the deal. No guns, boys. I want everyone to go to the front door of a different house. Check the door. If it is unlocked, open it. If it's not, look around for a hidden key. If you see or hear a person, dog, cat, anything, you haul ass back to the Escalade. Got it?" Dad is still looking around, but I can't figure at what.

"Sofie and Grace, you two stick together. Meet back here when you are done," he says, and Dad is out the door.

Dad is on his way to the furthest house. Sofie and Grace are walking up to the house where we are parked. We should have worked out who goes to which house in the car. I want to tell Liam that he should go to the house between Dad and Grace. I have this need to direct him and try and control him. But instead of saying anything, I start walking to the outside house.

In classic fashion, the basketball hoop distracts Liam. He

takes a couple of shots and dribbles a little before Dad's whistle snaps him awake. Then he heads on his way to the house between Dad and Grace.

My house is locked tight. There is no key to be found but the ADT security sticker is prominently displayed. I wonder if we need to worry about this. If I were the government looking for survivors, I would certainly tap into the ADT security network. It's odd to be thinking about breaking into a house and not be worried about getting in trouble. I am still worried. Maybe breaking and entering will always be the wrong thing to do?

We all meet back at the Escalade. Naturally Liam is the last one to get there. "Locked, no key." comes the report from Sofie.

"Mine too," I say.

"Same here," says Dad.

"Mine was locked, but I found a key." Liam is all smiles as if he did something to win this lottery.

"Were there any animals or strange noises inside?" Grace asks. I think she is hoping to find a cat or a parakeet or something.

"I didn't open the door. Dad only said to see if there was a key." Liam is looking puzzled. Even when he follows directions to the letter, he seems to find a way to have people annoyed with him.

"Seriously, Liam?" This can't surprise dad but he's looking at Liam in shock. Liam's hands are up in the air as if to say, *"What did I do?"*

"Seamus, go see if the key unlocks the door. Liam, Grace and Sofie, get anything you need for the night. We're staying here even if I have to use my key." The rock in his hand and the line out of a cheesy movie eventually have us all laughing. Except Dad doesn't laugh; apparently, he was serious.

The key works, of course. I step into the large foyer with a long, curving staircase to the second floor. The tile floor is clean and bright. On the left is a library/den/office—I'm not sure what you would call it. The room has floor to ceiling bookshelves, four large comfortable-looking chairs, and no obvious television screen or monitors. It looks as though no one has ever sat in that room, let alone recently. What a waste of resources to have a room full of stuff just for show.

On the right is a dining room. There is a long table that could seat fourteen. A gaudy reproduction sideboard completes the furniture in the room that I'm sure was called "elegant" or "stunning" by the homeowners' friends. Though I'm guessing they had more acquaintances, colleagues or associates. I can't imagine people who are this phony possibly having true friends.

I'm about to go straight where there is a hallway under the staircase when I feel a hand on my shoulder. My blood freezes and my legs become like cement. I don't know whether to run, callout or turn and face whoever it is. But I do nothing.

"Sorry to startle you, Seamus," Dad says as he walks past me with the gun in his hand. "Let me check the place out before we all go in. You wait here for the others. Same rules apply; if you hear anything out of the ordinary, haul ass back to the Escalade. Be ready to drive and get as far away as you can if anything comes out of the house other than me."

I didn't even realize he was whispering. My fear must have had all my sense at their peak performance. I'm not sure why Dad is suddenly being so clandestine. If there were a person or thing here, it would likely have attacked when the door opened. He's walking quietly but with purpose, doing his best impersonation of a SWAT team clearing a house.

Grace, Sofie and Liam arrive at the door and are annoyed with me for telling them to wait. But Dad is back at the foot of the stairs rather quickly. We don't have to argue for long, which is a relief. I am mentally exhausted from doing nothing.

"Sorry for weirding out there a little." Dad's voice is back to a normal level. "The first floor looks safe. Why don't you guys head back to the kitchen and living room area and investigate? I'm going to check the upstairs quickly, and I'll be down soon."

I don't understand why he can't communicate with us. He

is worried about something. It's obvious to me. Grace can probably tell that something is up but can't figure out who or what is out of whack. Liam is clueless, but I think Sofie can tell Dad's got something and won't let it go.

The rear of the house is gorgeous and gives a totally different impression of the people that lived here. It is an open floor plan with a large great room space on the left and a high-end but comfortable-looking cook's kitchen on the right. The great room has a big fireplace that looks well-used and the overstuffed couches and chairs look worn, comfortable and inviting. I can imagine them watching football games in the fall with family and friends while they cook and eat comfort food in the kitchen.

The back wall of the house is all windows. No, those look like they are actually doors. They open onto a patio that surrounds a pool and hot tub complex that is made for entertaining. Liam is already out there checking the water. Grace, Sofie and I head outside to join him.

Sneakers and socks are coming off fast, but it doesn't feel right. This isn't our house and we don't have permission. In the front of the house, I didn't care about these people. They were fake, mannequins. It didn't matter what we did here. Now that I've seen where they lived, the pictures on the wall, the comfortable relaxed atmosphere, I know they were a family, just like us. I'm thinking we should say a few words before anyone does a cannonball.

But I'm not the person for feelings. Why isn't Grace freaking about this? I can't even think of what I would say about these strangers. Nor can I muster the energy to stop the others from unwinding. We're working with a new norm, which is fine with me since I was never overly comfortable with the old norm. Maybe the others feel it, too. The energy has come way down and the expected progression to cannon balls and splashing fun hasn't happened. Now it seems like we've been sitting in silence for too long.

Dad comes walking out to the patio and is clearly agitated. "The pool looks really nice guys, but did anyone check for food and water? Potable water?" Now he is looking intently at each of us.

"I hate to be an ogre, but until we settle down somewhere, food and water need to be our top priority every time we stop for the night." Dad breaks the momentary silence. "Sofie and Grace, please go to the kitchen and inventory the food and water. See if there is anything in the freezer that we can eat tonight. If you find anything rotten or moldy, put it in a bag and we'll move it to the garage."

Everyone is slow to move. Dad is right, but now we all feel like 10 year olds who are in trouble for leaving our dirty clothes on the floor. The parent-child dynamic is back. Maybe this is a drawback of spending the night in a "family home."

"Liam, go see if you can work the entertainment system and if they have a library of DVDs or something so we can relax tonight." Dad is giving out busy-work so we don't fight or argue.

"Seamus, come with me. We need to tour the outside of the house." Dad's got a flashlight in the hand that previously held the gun. He's walking quickly towards the door in the back wall surrounding the patio. I take a breath to protest, but before I can speak, Dad starts talking: "Specifically I want you to look for a generator. If we lose power tonight, I want to make sure we can get it back, even if the grid is down."

Maybe thinking like a child has me feeling like a child. Dad clearly has some thoughts on what needs to happen to keep us safe and get everyone to California. Coaching myself not to feel chastised every time Dad raises a complaint will be tough. But I can do it. After all, I am not a mental midget.

A tour of the "perimeter," as Dad calls it, yields no generator. Dad points out a bush and a rock near the wall that could be used for a boost to get over the top. They bother him, but not nearly as much as not finding a generator. I hope he doesn't ask us to pack up so we can leave.

"Did you check the basement?" I ask him before the thought has even registered in my own head.

"Great idea, let's go." Dad is off.

The basement is neat and clean and well-organized. In what could only be called the "Systems Room" is a furnace and the hot water storage. There is also a pool heater unit and, there in the corner, is a generator. Everything runs off a central pipeline that is likely natural gas. I quickly inspect the generator and see that it is wired into the house's breaker panel and drives the breakers for the heat and water, as well as lights and outlets in the kitchen and great room. It's nice to see a breaker panel that is neat and well-labeled. I read the short instruction sheet on top and am confident that even Liam could turn on the generator in a matter of minutes if needed.

I can see and almost feel Dad's whole body relax. It has been a long day for him, but I think he is finally comfortable that we are safe and sound for the night. This is just the first day. I'm not sure if things will get easier or harder as we approach California, but I know Dad won't be able to maintain this level of functional-overstress for more than a few days.

When we get back upstairs, the party is in full swing. Music is playing in the kitchen, Grace is cooking something that smells amazing, and Sofie has opened a bottle of wine. Dad doesn't even ask who opened it or why; he just pours a big glass and heads out to the patio. Liam is doing cannonballs, going from pool to hot tub and back. Steam is being blown off in a big way. I stay in the kitchen and provide Grace a limited level of assistance.

I desperately want to ask where Sofie is. But Grace and I have been a team for so long, I need to maintain our bond. I need to make sure she knows that I am there for her. She and I are a part of each other's normal.

"You can go see Sofie if you want. She's in the hot tub." Grace is grinning knowingly and holding back her laugh.
"I'm good, thanks for offering." I smile back, and we start plating the meal.

CHAPTER 13

Dad went to bed right after dinner. He's always been the "early to bed, early to rise" kind of person. We were admonished not to stay up too late. While Dad went upstairs to a bedroom, we all dozed together in the great room. But now it's 5 a.m. and I am wishing I had gone to find a bed.

After another thirty minutes of restless rest, I can't stand it anymore. I'm going to get up and make a pot of coffee.

I should have known that Dad would already be awake. No complaints though; this way I don't have to make coffee. It's been a tough transition to black coffee now that we have no dairy products. I rummage through the cupboards looking for a non-dairy creamer to take the edge off, but no luck. I guess I'll have to grow some hair on my chest and deal.

Dad is sitting out by the pool and I pull up a chair next to him. Up through fourth grade, I would come downstairs in the morning and climb into Dad's lap and snuggle with him before school. I held onto that last little-boy act as long as could. It was safe and warm and comfortable and I want to climb onto his lap now. If I tried it today he would probably slap me and ask, "What the hell is wrong with you?" But it's because I'm 5'10" and 175 pounds, not because he doesn't want to snuggle.

"Beautiful sunrise." I finally break the silence.

"Well, it would be. If that were the east." Dad is defeated. He has no energy and the morning bounce he used to have is buried somewhere underneath a heavy wet blanket of worry.

After a few minutes, I'm still puzzled. "Sorry Dad, but what does that mean?"

"Sunrise, which will be around 7 a.m. at this time of year, comes from the east. It's a little after 5:30, and that light is coming from the west. That means something other than the sun is creating that beautiful glow." There is no pride or satisfaction in his explanation.

Could this be it? The government is sweeping the continent for survivors? The armed forces are moving methodically from the West coast to the East coast, and they aren't even stopping at night? That seems impractical. I have to start thinking smarter.

"Do you think something is scanning the planet?" I hate it when ideas like aliens take over my thoughts and make me speak. "Or maybe there was an explosion?" At least that seems a little more plausible.

"Ha-ha, aliens scanning the planet," Dad gives his nervous laugh. "Probably more along the lines of a wildfire."

It's funny that so many things burn but fire does not spontaneously occur in nature. With the exception of lightning strikes and volcanoes, people are usually needed to start a fire. The thing is that there are really no more people, left so how did this fire start? I suppose I have time to think about the different ways a fire could start while we drive.

"Are you going to shower this morning or just hop in the pool to freshen up?" Even in his glum state, Dad will be proud of me for being ready to move forward.

"Seamus, I don't know if I can do this." Dad is staring into the bottom of his empty coffee cup. "I am physically and mentally exhausted. It's like we are hit with one thing after another. I just want someone else to absorb a punch."

"Sofie and I can take shifts," I start before I am cut off with a sad, but surprised stare.

"You really haven't pieced it together?" He's searching my

face for a hint of realization. "That wildfire in the west is blocking our path to California. And as far as I can tell, it is heading this way fast. Driving is easy. Surviving this fire may be impossible."

"What if we leave in five minutes? We can drive around it." But he must have already thought about that and ruled it out.

"The only way south from here are back roads and minor highways. There is no way we could move fast enough to get around it." Dad is looking at a map only he can see and all the roads are dead ends.

"Then lets go north." I'm not thinking, just reacting.

"The lake is to the north. I'm not comfortable putting the five of us out there on a boat for who-knows-how-long with who-knows-what kind of weather coming. Seamus, I have thought about everything imaginable to get us out of here, and I'm blank." He's only been at it for fifteen minutes; how could he have given up so easily?

The silence is killing me. I want to brainstorm solutions with him, but he's not in the mood. In the background, I hear Sofie and Grace in the kitchen getting coffee. I'm not sure what it is, but I feel like there is a plan in the back of my mind and I need Grace to snap Dad out of his funk. Liam is still asleep, but that is not a surprise.

"Want more coffee?" I ask, getting up.

"Thanks." Dad slowly hands me his cup.

I meet the girls at the door and motion them back into the house.

"We have a big problem coming and a medium problem sitting on the pool deck," I tell them as we get over to the coffee maker. Both girls look out at Dad with an odd head tilt.

"I'm going to go work on solving the big problem. I need you to go work on Dad," I continue as they stare. "I need you to go out there and be sweet little Gracie. Dad needs to remember that he's not carting a bunch of junk across the country; he's taking care of his kids."

"What does that mean?" Grace is great at following

directions, except when she isn't clear on why she should follow them. This is what I am counting on.

"Just do it for me, please? I need him to remember how much he cares about us." That may have been over-the-top, but it should do the trick.

"Come with us then. I don't get what's happening and I want you to be there in case I need something explained." She is shuffling towards the patio and knows that I won't refuse to be there for her.

"Daddy, Seamus is worried about you and thinks you don't remember how much you care about us." Grace is pouty and sad.

I counted on this reaction from her. In fact, I could have written that down before she spoke and gotten it exactly right. Grace doesn't like deception, even when it is well-intentioned.

"What!? I care about you kids more than anything in the world." His spark isn't back, but maybe this small boost of adrenaline will help end his pity party.

"Sorry if I misunderstood our conversation, Dad." I need to shift gears and get things moving. "I'm going down to the basement to wire the generator to the irrigation system. I'm hoping that if we get enough water around and on us we can make it through that fake sunrise."

The plan in the back of my mind wasn't really much of a plan, more of an understanding of all the options that are off the table. Going around the fire is out based on speed and Lake Erie. Going over it is out based on none of us knowing how to fly. That leaves "sit tight and ride out the maelstrom." If Dad had even suggested we sit tight, I probably would have lost it on him.

The girls have puzzled looks on their faces, but I see a ray of hope in Dad's eye.

"I like the way you're thinking. Get it done and then go to the other three houses and do the same. Smash windows or whatever it takes to get in. Grace, go wake Liam. I'll explain everything in a minute." Dad is back. We're working on a level I never expected; it's intuitive. He can tell what I'm thinking and trying to accomplish. I know what parts he needs me to get done. I'm fascinated that impending death has us working more closely together than ever.

I'm off. No longer do I feel the need to hear and be involved in every second of planning. I trust that the others will execute their tasks. I need to execute mine.

My estimation is that it will take about fifteen minutes to move the breakers on the panel. Assuming all four houses in the cul-de-sac have generators, moving breakers at every house will take one hour to accomplish. I enjoy estimating how long it will take me to do certain tasks. I enjoy it even more when I'm right.

Standing in front of the breaker panel, it dawns on me that my father taught me to turn off power, replace a circuit breaker and even add a new circuit when I was 10. For two years, he required that I have him watch while I made changes to ours at home. By the time I was twelve, he let me make changes by myself. His only rule was that I had to be able to put things back the way they were after every change.

Flipping the power back on, I glance at my watch. Ten minutes, not bad. I'm going to leave the faceplate off. It's cosmetic anyway, and I don't have the time.

As I run up the stairs and out of the house, I realize that I did not include going between houses and breaking into them in my time estimate. Hopefully I can move each panel in ten minutes and use the extra five minutes between houses. The hammer I grabbed from the house we have taken over should help with getting into the other houses.

Smashing the hammer through the window feels really good. I didn't realize I had this aggression stored up. The fluidity between physical exertion and thoughtful action is rare to me. I like the effect it's having. Traditionally most of my thinking has occurred on the stool in my lab or sitting in the old recliner in front of the fire. Dad used to tell me that when I was stuck on something, getting out and moving around would shake loose the answer. I thought he was crazy, but maybe he was just using terms that don't suit me. Or maybe I didn't want to admit the old man might be right.

This house is laid out differently than next door. Finding the basement is still relatively easy. As I unscrew the faceplate of the breaker panel, I read down the labels to find the circuit for the irrigation system. Unlike the last house, it's labeled "sprinkler," which I get, but it means a different electrician wired this house.

The panel cover is off and I have eyes on the right circuit breaker. Oh shit, it's tripped! I'm actually not big on swearing, but this seems like a fair time to start.

Why is it tripped? Should I move it and then turn it back on or should I turn it back on first and see if a short trips it? Pre-apocalypse this would have been a long ordeal. Consultation with Dad, listing the possible reasons for the breaker to be tripped, an online search about wiring for irrigation systems, and on and on it would have gone. Today I just flip the breaker. It doesn't pop, which is good news. I look around the basement and find a Rain Bird Irrigation control center. Above it is a valve with a tag hanging from it. The handwritten tag reads "Open before activating sprinklers," but the valve is closed. It's October in Ohio. They freeze just like we do in New Hampshire. I don't even know if Dad has done it at home, but here they have already blown out and shut down the irrigation system. I need to make sure I get the system back online before I move any of the wiring. My time estimate is now out the window.

I don't like winging it, but that's what I've had to do with the irrigation system. The valve is open and I have turned the timer to "All Zones Manual On." I can hear water rushing through the pipes, but I have to go up to the yard and confirm that water is coming out of sprinkler heads.

Taking the stairs two at a time, I rush up from the basement. I rush through the front door to find my world in disarray. A Mercedes C-Class backs out from the garage of "our house". I see Dad at the wheel and he leaves an inch of rubber on the road before the car rockets off down the street. Liam is standing in the front yard with a can of gasoline and pouring it out on the grass. Not far from him I see a plumber's propane torch lying on its side. None of this makes any sense. How long was I in the basement?

"Liam! What the hell are you doing? Pretty soon we are going to have more fire than we can handle." I swore again and I'm afraid I could get use to it.

"I'm making a reverse fire thing." Liam is looking at me like I am the one doing something crazy.

"I have no idea what a reverse fire thing is. You're such an idiot, are you trying to help us live or help us die?" The sprinklers are sputtering to life, but I have to deal with my brother.

"Remember we saw that thing about forest fires on TV and they dug a trench and burned everything before the fire got there?" He's making digging motions with his hands as if the digging was the key takeaway.

"It's called a backfire and if you can't remember the name, how can you possibly remember how to execute it safely, not to mention correctly?" My exasperation is lowering now that I know his intent. If we burn all the fuel around the cul-de-sac, the fire may spare us as it looks for more to burn.

"Seamus, I'm not an idiot. Just because I'm different from you doesn't make me worthless. I don't remember names or how to calculate how much gas I need to burn up a yard. But I get how it's supposed to work and I know I can do it." Liam is defensive, but he's never stated his case this calmly and clearly before.

"Liam, that's fine, I'm not saying you're worthless. But you can't screw this up, it's our lives at stake!" I don't have much of a choice. It's a good idea, but I don't have time to do it and get all the irrigation systems going.

"Seamus, Mom always said that we fight because we're brothers and that when we grow up we'll get along great and know how to trust each other. I think it's time we grow up. You need to trust me." He leaves it at that and goes back to work.

I have no basis for trusting him. There are four iPods, two

cell phones, a tablet, and countless video games, shoes, hats and more that he has lost or forgotten. There is not a negative or malicious bone in his body; Liam is genuinely a good person. But trusting him with our lives is a tough pill to swallow.

With that, I am off to the basement to move the irrigation breaker to the generator slot on the panel. If I can get this one and the next two houses done quickly, I can help Liam with the backfire.

CHAPTER 14

We are all sitting in the great room quietly, waiting for chaos, insanity and a wall of fire to shock us into action. Dad insisted we all eat something and drink water. When the fire gets here, we will need all the energy we can muster just to survive. There will be no time to refuel.

It took almost an hour to get the other two houses done. Both houses on the outside of the cul-de-sac had their generators and irrigation systems installed after the houses were built. That meant that the controls for them were not together, so I had to deal with some running around to get things right.

Liam's backfire seems to work great. There is scorched earth all around the cul-de-sac. I can't see anything left that is flammable, with the exception of the houses. The fleeing Mercedes carried Dad and Sofie. They returned in a ladder truck from the local fire department. Dad says he intends to do his best to flood the patio and hide the house behind a curtain of water.

The temperature just rose what feels like fifty degrees in a heartbeat. Dad walks across the patio to the wall and peers out the back gate. He becomes very animated as he steps out into the yard. I don't know when it started, but the wind is blowing fiercely and there is a demonic howl rising above a low roar making it difficult to hear. Dad is yelling something towards me, but I can't hear him.

We have regular garden sprinklers mounted on the top of the wall, with the hoses connected to the house faucet. They are on, but the wind is whipping the water into fine mist. It looks like we are trying to put out a bonfire with a tiny plant mister.

Dad is closer now and I can hear him. The sprinklers are not working. This was my part of the plan. The sprinklers are what brought Dad back from quitting and I screwed them up.

I run with Dad to the back gate and peer out. It is intensely hot. There is water flowing at the house next to us in the middle of the cul-de-sac. But our house and the two on the ends are dry. I'm already running when I say to Dad, "You fix ours. I'll get the other two."

The fire has already reached the edge of Liam's back-burn. The fire hose is keeping things wet, but even that volume of water feels insignificant compared with the tidal wave of molten flame.

In the garage of the neighboring house, I flip the irrigation controller to "All Zones On Manual" and hear the water rush through the system. I can't believe I left the sprinkler system off. My stupidity may contribute to the death of my family.

Flaming debris is raining from the sky. It's like we're in a fire tornado. Three houses have their sprinklers on in a futile attempt to keep the flames at bay. I'm not sure I can even make it back to our house, let alone over to the final house to activate that sprinkler system.

As I run for the back gate of our house, the roof of the house I just left catches fire. It won't be long before it is completely gone. I'm guessing the temperature is at or over 200 degrees. If we don't burn, we may bake to death.

When I'm steps from our gate, the far house, the one with no sprinklers running, explodes. I'm knocked to the ground and completely disoriented. I still need to get over there and turn on the sprinklers. But I know it's a futile effort; the sprinklers are gone. As I get to my feet though, I am drawn to complete my mission. Slowly I get my bearings and stagger towards the crater that was someone's home.

A set of large hands grabs me by the shoulders and begins dragging me backwards. My skin feels like it's on fire. The hands are not comforting. They are coarse and rough and hold me too tightly. I'm not being saved; I am being deterred from my goal. In my mind I am thrashing and fighting, but my feet come into focus and I see them perfectly still, dragging across concrete. It's quiet and bright. I'm not sure what we were so afraid of. This is nice.

The cold water steals the air from my lungs. My senses come rushing back and as I burst through the surface of the pool I hear a deafening roar, the opposite of quiet. Between my gasps and coughing, I hear my name screamed.

"Seamus! Are you all right? I thought you died! I thought we lost you!" Grace is in overload. I can tell that she is screaming at the top of her lungs, but I can barely hear her. The noise is deafening. The sensory inputs are overwhelming.

As I survey the scene, I am at awe of nature. Grace, Sofie and Liam are in the shallow end of the pool with me. We are all standing in water up to our waist and dripping wet. There is an intense orange and red glow surrounding the house. I can't actually see flames, but it looks like we are inside of a flame. The wind is still whipping and burning debris and soot are falling from the sky in a blizzard. The heat is immense and barely tolerable. It won't be long before we need to submerge up to our necks. Will the hot air burn our lungs as we inhale?

After I complete my childlike survey of our environment, Grace snaps me back to the present by pounding on my chest. She is screaming my name repeatedly, but has nothing to say. Sofie is standing alone, sobbing with a distant look in her eye, likely in shock. Liam is staring at Grace and me, unsure of his role in our piece of the family dynamic.

"The Escalade!" I blurt out. We spent so much time preparing the house that we forgot about our whole world. The car and the last remaining vestiges of "us" are in the driveway next to the fire truck. It's as if we considered them animate objects, that the fire truck would actively watch over and protect its young offspring, the SUV.

Before I can reach out and stop him, Liam is up the steps of the pool and running for the house. I don't know where he is going, but if he dies in the Escalade I will not live long myself, knowing my words sent him there.

I've lost all sense of time. Upon realizing this I understand that I am regaining an awareness of time. I'm not sure how long I have been in the pool, or how long Liam has been gone, but I know Dad is not present in the water.

The wind and the noise have either come down in intensity or my hearing has adapted to the cacophony. I shout to Grace and Sofie who are now wrapped in a feeble embrace with me. "Where's Dad?"

Grace seems to have stopped functioning. She worries for others when they stub their toe. The worry and concern she must feel right now has drained her.

"He's manning the fire truck," Sofie hollers back. She keeps splashing water on her face. I'm sure it's to keep cool but it also has the effect of washing away the dirt and tears. Her face is drained of energy and emotion, but her beauty is still radiant. This hardly seems like the time to be thinking about falling in love, but I can't stop.

Leaning over slowly, I kiss her. I have no explanation for this action. It is unwarranted and inappropriate. But she's kissing me back! This is amazing. In thirty years, will our children believe the story of our first kiss? I think not. It dawns on me that I'm not sure if this is a first kiss or a last kiss. Was this a final act of desperation before we all die? Or is this a first act of resolution that we will defend and protect each other until the end of time?

My romantic interlude is stunted when the back end of the Escalade comes crashing through the house. As the girls and I dive into the water for cover, the brakes engage. When we surface, we see the giant SUV skid to a stop just short of the pool. There are dings and dents, scratches and burn marks everywhere. Our luxury land liner looks like the battle-wagon Sofie had declared it to be.

I can see Liam come around the front of the truck to the passenger side. I can't imagine how hot it is or feels up there. The girls and I stand motionless, watching as if we are at some strange swim-up movie theatre. The door opens and Dad slumps out of the car onto Liam's shoulders. Liam is not big, maybe 5'8" when he lets his hair grow, and 140 pounds after a big meal. He's diminutive compared to Dad's 6'1", 220 pounds. But Liam is tenacious, and he manages to drag Dad over to the pool.

Standing on the edge, they both just fall into the water. No effort or control. One last act from two people that have no energy left to act. Sofie and Grace are to Dad almost before he is even underwater. I let Liam submerge and float for a moment. Part of me expects him to do a somersault and surface with a mouthful of water to spit in my face. But we're not swimming for fun. I reach down and pull him to the surface.

"Thanks Seamus." I see the words move through his lips. It's still too loud to hear each other and he is in no position to shout.

I half-swim, half-float him to the pool stairs. The girls and I sit Liam and Dad down on the stairs in water up to their necks. Dad is barely conscious and Grace needs to hold his head up to keep him from face-planting into the water. Liam can keep himself upright, but I have my arm around him in case that changes suddenly.

Water from the fire hose splashes off the roof of the Escalade and showers down on top of us. Although it feels like it, we are not on fire. One more explosion indicates the loss of a second house on the cul-de-sac. In a surreal sight, there are patches of the roof of our house on fire, even as water from the fire truck streams down around them.

There is no way we can survive if the temperature rises further. These thoughts are taking longer and longer to form. My brain is shutting down critical thinking and diverting all power to survival. I have become the basest form of human life: heart beating and lungs pumping, nothing else worthy of energy or thought.

We are all lost in a similar catatonic state. The duration is unknown, but I am registering a drop in temperature. Life would be bearable if I moved to the top step of the pool, so I do. Soon I am on the pool deck. I lie face-down in the sooty, tepid water. I want to cry, but despite all of the water, I am dehydrated. I look up to see Sofie and Grace helping Dad and Liam onto the pool deck.

The wind and the rage of the fire have gone. There is an eerie stillness and silence as Sofie walks slowly towards me.

"Grace is going to stay with Liam and your Dad. I need you to help me get some bedding and dry clothes." She is persuading me, no commands or demands. I need to muster the energy to do this with her.

As I rise to my feet, critical thinking comes back slowly. I realize the irony that after having just survived an hours-long wild fire ordeal, we could freeze to death tonight if we don't have dry clothes and bedding.

CHAPTER 15

I wake up with a headache, which is not surprising but is still not comfortable. Looking outside through the blown-out window, it is still dark. My watch, a gift for my 10th birthday, did not survive the fire. For a few summers I gave that watch a pretty good beating. I always thought it was indestructible. It's another reminder of how close we must have come to not making it.

No one else is awake. Everyone is together in what had been the library or den of the house. We sleep on makeshift beds and are covered with an assortment of blankets and tarps. If it weren't for the snoring and the modern furnishings, we could be mistaken for sarcophagi arranged around a burial chamber.

Grace was the last one to lie down. It was like she was tucking everyone in. She made sure we all had a water bottle and ample covers. Her people skills are amazing. She made everyone feel safe, secure and comfortable, but did not make it seem like we were being "mothered." I drift back to sleep, thinking that we couldn't have made it through the fire if any one of us had been absent.

As I sleep, I dream of jumping on the trampoline. My body is younger, maybe 8 years old, but my mind is current and aware of everything. I'm all alone on the trampoline, and it feels so good to have this time and space to myself. It makes me really happy and warm inside. This is strange because I no longer crave that alone time like I did when I was younger. The last week has been spent in close quarters with my family and Sofie. In the past, I would have been dying to get away and have some privacy, but not now. Now I welcome the closeness and support of these special people.

My dreaming turns to the reactor. I haven't really thought about it for almost two days—the longest hiatus since I began working on it. But why am I running through the components and requirements? The design is done. My computer simulation completed. I know it will work; I am just waiting to build it. The only outstanding issue is connecting it to the power grid, which is not technically a problem for the reactor, so why am I dreaming about it? Is this a problem I subconsciously solved when I was eight?

Grace and Liam are climbing into the trampoline now. As much as I just acknowledged their value and importance to me, I want to get out. This is my time. I'm solving problems here; give me some space. But they won't leave. In fact, they are both getting closer, until they grab me and start pushing me. I raise my hands to push them away and startle awake. Grace is staring down at me with a smile. Liam is watching her, trying to judge how he is supposed to react.

"Morning, sleepyhead. Dad wants us to get up so we can get on the road." Grace is standing now and surveying the room.

As I get to my feet, the room is a disturbing sight. The windows are blown out. There is water dripping all around us. Debris and soot litters the floor. I have no idea how all this stuff got in here, but if any one piece had been any hotter, landed in a slightly different place or not passed through the wall of water, the house would have burned to the ground.

We've walked back to the great room, empty-handed. There is nothing worth taking with us. Out by the pool Dad and Sofie are cleaning off the Escalade. Thanks to Liam it survived, but it is definitely worse for wear. I know Dad is going to want to replace it, but after that fire there cannot be another vehicle around for hundreds of miles.

Without much discussion we all climb into the battlewagon and find our seats. There is nothing to pack up. What little we had unpacked is in tatters in the shell of the house. The planning we did for the fire did not include plastic bags to keep our things safe from the water. I don't know how far reaching the fire was but the only resources we have left in the world are stuffed in the back of the Escalade.

Dad slowly pulls through the hole in the back wall of the garage. I'm not sure if he is worried about nails or other debris popping the tires, but it doesn't seem like it. He is indiscriminately rolling over piles of debris. As we get out to the cul-de-sac, the road is dirty but does not appear to be blocked by anything large.

We ride along in silence, surveying the wasteland around us. Was it just two days ago that this was green countryside? Now I am reminded of the pictures from history class that showed Hiroshima and Nagasaki after the nuclear bombs were dropped.

While we had all been aware of the loss of humans, it didn't *feel* like we were living in a post-apocalyptic world. Now all that has changed. I know it was a wildfire, but the result gives the distinct impression that two superpowers waged an historic battle. As if mutually assured destruction was acceptable as long as it was complete. We were not meant to survive any of this; yet here we are, limping along the last vestiges of I-80.

"Can we call Mom?" Liam breaks the silence from the back seat. Liam always breaks the silence, but this time I cannot complain.

"That's a good idea," Dad says as he hands his phone back to Grace.

We are bouncing along at 40 miles per hour. The trash in the road and the effect the fire had on the tires has greatly diminished our top speed. We lost a day in the fire and now we will lose more days having to drive slowly. I thought we could get to California early, but now it seems we will be days late. I haven't worried about Mom in a while. But now I'm worried that she'll be mad at us when we reset expectations for our arrival. We should have left sooner.

Grace seems to be having trouble with the phone, but I can't imagine what it is. I look over at her with a puzzled look. She's showing me the phone and it's the call history screen. It's full of calls to Mom from yesterday. She flicks the screen and Mom's name appears over and over again. Well, over one hundred times, but I can't tell if Dad ever got through. Did they speak? Did he leave a message? Was he trying to say goodbye, assuming the worst from the fire?

"There is no signal at all." Grace isn't really talking to anyone in particular.

We haven't seen any utility poles in the past few hours of driving. There haven't even been the tall radio towers that are so commonly visible on cross-country journeys. It's no wonder there is no cell signal. The towers must have fallen over or at least the equipment was destroyed in the forest fire.

"Phone equipment is designed to withstand the hottest summer temperatures and even electronic charges caused by lightning strikes. When I worked at Cisco, we had a lab where they tested equipment for use in the field. It was pretty cool." Dad doesn't usually reminisce about the days when he worked.

"I bet none of it was designed to withstand a wildfire," Liam says. The telephone network was built tough and designed to last, but it was not indestructible.

Suddenly I feel the brakes engage and the Escalade slows to a stop.

"Sofie, would you mind driving for a while? I need a rest." Dad is looking over at Sofie.

"No problem," she replies and they are both opening their doors as if this had been planned. I'm too tired to be offended that I was not considered as a driver. Plus I need to set my brain to work solving some other problems.

"Just keep it at or under forty okay?" Dad is in the

passenger seat, settling in.

"Got it." Sofie already has the car in drive and we are moving forward.

I need to focus on this morning's dream. I'm convinced that I have the answer to a key question. The problem is that I don't even know what the question is, so I can't think about the answer. It's even worse than that. If I make myself dream, do I focus on the trampoline or do I focus on connecting the reactor to the grid?

As exhaustion is setting in throughout the car, I also realize that we need to find a place to stay tonight. I have no doubt that there will be no mansion. Forget about luxury hotels; from the looks of things there won't even be a Red Roof Inn or budget hotel tonight. We can always sleep in the Escalade, but that would not be restful and I can imagine that one of us would wind up killing Liam.

Sofie winds up driving for hours. My mind is shifting back and forth between power grid connectors and what type of shelter may have survived the fire, until finally Sofie applies the brakes and stops.

"Enough. I have no idea how you do it but I cannot drive another mile," she says. The door is open and Sofie is climbing out. She stands up tall and then bends over to touch her toes. She's flexing her legs and hopping around before she goes right into jumping jacks.

Dad leans across the console and turns off the ignition. There's a big smile on his face and he turns to us in the back of the car. "Sofie has a great point. Let's all get out and stretch a little bit."

The three of us pile out of the back of the truck. Grace and Sofie immediately join up and start comparing stretches and yoga exercises. Liam somehow has a football with him and throws it over to Dad.

I play catch with Liam and Dad for a little bit. It's an interesting and well-deserved interlude, but I'm ready for it to be over.

"Liam, go deep!" Dad shouts and Liam takes off running

on I-80 West. Dad throws a bomb and Liam runs under it, making a perfect basket catch.

After a few more deep routes, I feel like we need to move on.

"How are we fixed for gas?" I ask, in an effort to get our minds back on moving forward.

The wobble that replaces Dad's perfect spiral is all the answer I need. Not good.

"We have about 94 miles to empty and it doesn't seem likely that we'll find a surviving gas station in those miles." Dad has regained his spiral, but the long throws are done.

Grace and Sofie have stopped stretching and doing yoga. The three of us are staring at Dad. We forgot about gas. If we run out of gas, there will be no choice but to sleep in the Escalade tonight. And then walk tomorrow. The barren landscape makes walking feel like a very exposed position, fraught with risk.

"What are you guys talking about?" Liam is now back with us by the truck.

"Gas." I'm not trying to sound mean, but with Liam it comes naturally.

"Liam, I don't know if we are going to find a gas station before the car runs out." Dad is not happy with me giving attitude.

"What are those things called at gas stations, you know like the upside down U?" Liam is motioning in the air with his hands, making an upside down U, as if the communication problem is that none of us can picture the shape.

"You have to be kidding me with this, Liam!" I growl and spin around, a physical display of my frustration.

"No, you know those things at the ends of the pumps? It's like a thick pipe in an upside down U shape and they go into the ground," he's on the ground showing us the thickness of the pipe with his hands and gesturing how it would come up out of the ground.

"I'm sorry, buddy, but I have no idea what you're talking about. But why does it matter anyway?" Dad is ready to shift back to defeat.

"Because I've seen them." He doesn't understand why we aren't following him and is getting excited.

"What do you mean you've seen them? If they're at gas stations, we've all seen them." Sofie is getting in on it.

"Well, while we have been driving today I was watching for patterns." A smile is growing across Liam's face. "I noticed the first one right after we got on the highway this morning. I've seen three more since then but it's been awhile since I saw the last one. So I think another one is coming up."

"You mean you think you can find a gas station?" Sofie is the first one with a trace of optimism in her voice.

"Yup." Triumphant Liam is one of my least favorite Liam's.

CHAPTER 16

Liam had been right. The concrete and steel barriers that protect the pump islands from reckless and distracted drivers had the right combination of materials and size to partially survive the fire. Once we began intently surveying the landscape and searching for clues that would indicate a gas station, it seemed obvious when we came to one.

Fortunately we had the pump and hoses from the gas station experience back home. It took awhile to find the covers for the underground tanks, but we were able to find the fuel and eventually get the Escalade filled.

We have been on the road for well over 12 hours now. The sun has fallen out of the sky and darkness is chasing away the dusk quickly. I know Dad does not want to travel at night, but there has been no discussion of stopping.

"Is that a river?" Sofie is pointing out the front window.

"I think I see a tree!" Grace shouts.

"We made it." Dad lets out a sigh.

"Made what?" Sofie is getting a lesson in Dad's poor communication.

"The Mississippi river. We'll stop on the other side," he answers solemnly.

As we approach the river, the effects of the fire seem to

lessen. While I know it isn't true, I think the fire had intelligence. It saw the river and knew there was no way across. Instead of raging against that barrier and consuming all the fuel right up to the waters edge, it receded and headed east, where it was unfettered until it reached the Atlantic. It burned ruthlessly consuming towns and cities, Chicago, Philadelphia, New York and Boston. I can't say for certain, but it feels as if half of the United States was wiped away.

Dad doesn't stop at the bridge. He rolls right on over it. As if we are desert travelers arriving at an oasis after a day baking in the sun, we cheer when we reach the other side. We're back to civilization and humanity. There are buildings and billboards, trees and grass. Things are looking up, and I can feel the energy in the car.

While we are still adjusting back to the world we are used to, we see a sign proclaiming "The County's Top Cadillac Dealer" four miles ahead. The next sign brings more good news: a Holiday Inn at the same exit, complete with Wi-Fi, a restaurant and an indoor pool. There is no way Dad can pass this up. These were put here together, just for us.

"We'll stay at that Holiday Inn tonight. In the morning, we can get new tires or move into a completely new Escalade." Dad didn't let me down.

"Wow, Paddrick Robinson takes the easy route. Mark this day on the calendar." Sofie is grinning from ear to ear and we all crack up at her jab.

"Oooh, a Cracker Barrel. I love Cracker Barrel," Grace is caught up in the moment. But we all fade quickly to silence. We survived the fire. The exhilaration of making it to the clean, undamaged, *whole* side of the river helped us to forget our reality.

The ugly truth is everywhere though. There are no other cars on the road. There are no people to be seen anywhere. We could go to the Cracker Barrel, but it's not there anymore. There is a building with a sign on it and stuff inside, but not the people who make it a restaurant. There are no cooks, servers or cashiers. The manager won't greet us at the door with a smile and "*Welcome to Cracker Barrel.*" Fast food, or even good food, quickly is becoming a part of our past. In our present, food needs to be thought about and worked for.

As we turn down the exit ramp, Grace's phone rings. The bubbly pop ditty startles all of us, and she has to look at the device awkwardly for a moment before realizing what is happening.

"Hello?" The single word tentatively comes out of her mouth.

"Mom!" Tears are streaming down her face and she is sobbing between fits of laughter. "No, we're okay. There was a fire and it was wicked bad. The car was really banged up and we had to drive slower all day today." The words are choked out in fits and starts. I can't imagine that Mom really understands it too well. "Here's Liam." Grace finishes her conversation and hands the phone to the back seat.

"Hi Mom. How's California?" It's as if he doesn't understand that things are different now, but it's Liam—he may not. "Yeah, the house had a cool pool with a hot tub. We stayed in the water and were okay. Today I played football with Dad and Seamus and then I helped find gas." Liam does not dwell, reflect on, or learn from the past. At times that seems like a strength; other times, not so much. "I love you, too. See you soon. And oh, here's Seamus."

"Hi Mom. I love you." I feel good to be able to say it to her.

"Are you okay?" she asks, as if she wouldn't have heard otherwise from the other two.

"I'm fine. We all worked together as a team and made it through. You don't need to worry about us, we'll tell you all the stories when we get to San Francisco." Now is not the time to relay the terror we survived. "I can't wait to see you. Here's Dad." I rush because the connection could drop at any time and Dad needs this as much as we do.

Dad pulls the Escalade under the portico at the Holiday Inn. He slowly puts it in park and turns off the ignition while tilting his head back and letting out a deep breath as his head gently reaches the head rest.

"Hey babe," I hear him say as the rest of us pile out of the SUV.

There is still power here, and the four of us walk through the automatic sliding doors and into the lobby. We've all stayed in hotels before, but we stand in awe for a moment. Compared to what we woke up in this morning and what we spent the day driving through, this is the Palace at Versailles.

"Has anyone ever worked the front desk of a hotel?" Sofie has no idea that none of us has ever held a real job.

"No, but I bet there is an instruction sheet near the machine that activates the key cards. It can't be too hard." I have confidence that I can figure out how to use any computerized system.

Sofie and I walk around the front desk while Grace and Liam head to the snack shop. I hope they inventory the water and identify any supplies that would be useful for replenishing what we consumed today. I hear a soda can crack open while I'm looking for any type of instruction sheet. I guess it's okay to have a refreshment while you work; no need to get into it with Liam.

It's not as obvious as I expected. I've seen them make the keys before. They type in a few digits, wait a moment, type a few more digits, then swipe a card. My guess is that the first few digits unlock or activate the system. The second set of digits is the room number, and the card swipe is self-explanatory. We just need the unlock code.

Sofie's search takes her into a back room and out of my sight. I don't like having her out of my view, and a chill rushes down my spine. "Sofie," I call out as I walk to the back room.

It only takes a few seconds for me to get there, and she's obviously fine, but I feel better being able to look at her. She's leaning on a desk, studying a corkboard full of flyers, memos and post-it notes. I pause for a moment to study the curve of her body. My mind is consumed by the beauty of her face. Memory of the kiss we shared in the pool washes over me and sets my heart racing.

"When you're done staring, I could use a hand looking for a code or something that will help us get into the rooms." Her gaze hasn't left the board, but I see one corner of her mouth turn up slightly in a smirk.

"What's going on in here?" Dad calls from the lobby.

Grace is the first to answer. "We're taking an inventory of the water and collecting supplies to replace what we used today."

"What about Seamus and Liam?" He assumed that Grace and Sofie would be working together.

"Liam is with me, " Grace starts to say.

"Got it!" Sofie's exclamation interrupts. In a flash, she moves from the office to the key card machine. There is a key in her hand and she is about to enter the code.

"Hold on. What room are you going to program?" Dad is standing at the counter like an unhappy, demanding customer.

"I don't know, one of these on the top floor, maybe 820?" Sofie is defensive, but I can tell from her face she's not sure why.

"Seamus, can you get into the computer and see if there are some vacant rooms?" Dad isn't mad, but he has something on his mind.

"I don't think there is anyone who will mind if we take their reservation," Sofie chuckles nervously.

"It's just that I think we should try to avoid rooms that were listed as occupied before everyone got sick." Dad looks uncomfortable and his speech is uneasy.

Walking in on a corpse would be disturbing. The sickness hit so fast that people who were traveling just died in their hotels. There are likely hundreds of dead bodies in this hotel, and I see another reason Dad opted for a private residence last time we stopped. I'm wondering why there is no odor of decay, but stop abruptly. I'm going to try and be grateful for it without analyzing.

"Here we go. There are blocks of rooms on two, six and seven. Sorry Sofie, the 8th floor is occupied." I'm doing my best impression of a hotel clerk to try and restore some lightness to the mood.

"Make a few keys for the block on two and let's get settled in. I'm starving and exhausted, and I want to take a long shower." Dad is talking over his shoulder as he walks to the snack shop.

I want to recommend that we move to a higher floor for defensive purposes. It would show that I am learning and thinking more strategically for the new world we live in. But I hold my tongue. Dad was very specific, and I bet he has a reason for picking the second floor. I just have to figure out what it is.

When we get to the second floor, Dad surveys each room and specifically checks the windows. He's not really looking out, but more looking around as if he were interested in the window itself and not what was on the other side.

"Seamus, you and Liam go down to the maid's closet. Get a screwdriver. And Liam, you get all the extra sheets you can carry." The inspection is over, but we have not been given permission to settle in.

"Dad, come on. You have to tell us what you're thinking. From where we stand, this seems crazy." I'm not really standing up to him, but I am standing up for us.

"Yeah" and "please" come back from the other three.

"In case something happens or somehow we are not alone, I want to make sure we can get out these windows and safely to the ground." He looks intently at each of us. "I don't mean to alarm you, but I also don't want to have to figure this out in the middle of some type of emergency."

Strangely, this won't help me sleep easier tonight. It makes sense, but not in a comforting *"we'll be okay"* kind of way. It's more of a *"be afraid, things could go south fast"* kind of feeling.

CHAPTER 17

We all needed the good night's sleep. I love being asleep for upwards of twelve hours straight. It really recharges my batteries, in a different way from getting 6-to-8 hours of sleep. It's after 9:30. I'm surprised but glad Dad hasn't woken everyone up to get the day going.

Grace, Liam and I migrated en masse to the kitchen downstairs. We didn't wake Dad or Sofie, and there was no discussion; we just quietly left and headed downstairs. I think that if a psychologist were alive they would be fascinated by our behavior. Our actions were normal for pre-apocalypse life, until we got to the restaurant. We headed straight to the kitchen and began rummaging through the shelves and refrigerators for food, as if ransacking a kitchen was a common, everyday occurrence.

Previously we had all agreed that eggs were generally safe. Liam cracked a dozen into a bowl and began beating them for scrambled eggs. Grace opened some cans of fruit and put together a fruit salad. Being non-domestic myself, it was all I could do to make toast and find some butter to slap on it. There is still no milk, but we have coffee, orange juice and water to drink.

It's fun. We are just eating, talking and walking around the kitchen exploring. There is no pressure or stress. It's like a weird brunch at a stranger's house. The three of us haven't had time like this since the beginning of the summer. After the last few weeks, we need it almost as much as we needed the sleep.

When Dad walks in with Sofie, we all realize there is probably something else we could have been doing. Or maybe we should have woken them so we could have gotten on the road. It feels like there is so much that we should be doing at all times it's impossible to make a decision that doesn't make me feel bad for not doing enough.

"Is there any food left?" Sofie is helping herself to coffee and grabbing a plate.

"I want some eggs, and bacon would be magnificent." Dad gets his coffee and plate after Sofie.

Liam scoops some eggs onto their plates and drops another pound of bacon in the griddle. I get myself some more coffee and Grace just looks around smiling.

"So listen. After we eat, we need to get moving." Dad has a schedule in his head. I'm hoping he'll share more than "get moving."

"After I woke up, I ran across the street to the dealer. I thought about just swapping wheels from a new car to our car, but I don't think that's the smart move. So I got a new Escalade and we need to move all of our stuff and get it fueled up." He breaks for a long drink of coffee. I have no idea how he can drink coffee when it is so scalding hot.

"Bacon's up," Liam the short-order cook chimes in.

As if to remind us that we need to get moving, the power goes out before Dad even takes a bite of his bacon. Our brief hiatus from hell is over; this is not a vacation.

"It's about 10:45 now." Dad looks at his watch. "I want to be on the road by noon. If we do this right, we can be in California tomorrow night." He grabs a piece of bacon and puts the whole thing in his mouth.

Grace and I are done eating, so we each grab another coffee and head up to start working on the car swap. I know it's selfish, but I am focused on the best way to move both of my rooftop carriers. I would love to come up with a way of doing it without unpacking them, but they are heavy. I also don't want to drop them and damage the few tools I have left.

Grace opens the back of the old battlewagon. She likes to do things, not analyze them. "Hold on," I tell her. I want to park them as close together as possible. That will make it easier to move the roof carriers and easier to move the stuff inside. I pull the new ride alongside the old one and slowly bring the doors together until I hear the scraping sound. Satisfied that the two are as close as possible, I climb over the console and get out the rear passenger side door.

By the time I get my first rooftop carrier disconnected, Dad, Liam and Sofie are there and helping.

We are on the road a little before noon. Dad is pleased with our efficiency and the fact that we are ahead of schedule. The average speed is quickly up over 100 miles per hour and it feels like there is nothing that can get in our way now.

We have a quick early pit stop after all that coffee, but then we are back on the road. After the wasteland from yesterday, today's travel is decidedly un-apocalyptic. There are movies and music and singing. Spirits are high; tomorrow night we'll see Mom.

After about six hours of driving, Dad slows the car to a stop.

"Bio break," he shouts as he hops out the door and runs to the edge of the highway. We all take the cue and exit the vehicle to stretch and empty our bladders. It's late afternoon and the autumn air is light and crisp, and it has me feeling uneasy. This is just how horror movies start.

"Are we going to stop for the night soon?" Liam is anxious to be done with driving for the day.

"That's probably not a bad idea. Something doesn't feel right to me." Grace is being affected by the environment the same way I am.

"No. I'd like to go for another three hours at least." Dad leaves no room for discussion. "The driving is easy and the further we get tonight, the less we have to go tomorrow."

It's a good point, but he is the one that has us all afraid of traveling in the dark. Maybe if I call Mom she can convince him to break for the day and take extra time if we need it. A quick look at my phone finds no bars, just as it's been all day.

We just passed a road sign that said we were in North Platte, Nebraska. I know that Wyoming is next and that means mountains and possibly snow. Maybe he'll agree to stop before we start up the Rockies.

"Mount up, let's go." Dad is in the car and we all join him without argument.

He drops the hammer and the Escalade shoots off and gets back to 100 miles per hour in a flash. I close my eyes to focus on changing Dad's mind about stopping for the night. Instead, the noise and rhythm of the road send me right off to sleep. It's a deep and sound sleep, but I'm not aware of any dreams.

I'm not sure if it was the explosion or my head slamming into the window that woke me up, but I am alert now. I can feel the car skidding sideways. This is not a fishtail; it is total loss of control. My eyes find Dad and see a calmness and serenity I didn't expect. He is working the steering wheel hard but without panic. Years of driving in snow and practicing skids and loss of control are proving beneficial. If it had been Sofie or me behind the wheel, there is no doubt the car would have flipped and left us all on our heads.

Grace is screaming and Sofie is howling, while in the back Liam just keeps saying "Dad," over and over again. As far as I know, I am silent.

The impact is abrupt and the deceleration complete, immediate. The seat belt has done its job, but not without side effects and complications. The side curtain airbag deployed but I didn't feel it. I expect it was more cosmetic than functional. We were probably traveling at about 70 miles an hour when whatever it was got in our way. I want to tell Dad that this is why we shouldn't have been traveling at night, but it seems impossible to see through the fog.

Twice in two days now I have been blown into a mental

fog by an explosive event. I've seen the concussion studies and I know this is not good for my body or brain. I need to get moving, check to make sure the others are okay. But what do I do if they are not okay? I have no medical training. Not even basic first aid. From movies and television, I know to put pressure on a bleeding wound, but how do you treat internal injuries? Broken bones? Lack of consciousness?

Slowly I get myself together. There are no big hands to pull me to safety this time. I decide to open the door and get out of the SUV to assess our situation. It's dark out, but the sky is clear and the moonlight helps illuminate my surroundings. My feet land on pavement and I can see that we did not leave the highway during the crash. Tractor-trailer trucks are parked on both sides of the road. But they are not parked carelessly. They are aligned end to end, forming a wall. Now I see one across the highway where we just came from. How did Dad get around that? Or is that why we crashed?

I look to the front of the Escalade and see that the grill is stuffed into the side of a large bulldozer. It doesn't make a lot of sense to me. There are no other signs of construction, and even if the operator was working when he got sick, it seems an odd place to abandon this piece of equipment. In the other lane but further down the road is another bulldozer. Just like this one, it is parked across the lanes of traffic, almost as if it were meant to be a roadblock.

A roadblock? I spin around, far too quickly for my injured brain. Dizziness overcomes me and I fall against the car. I'm not steady on my feet but my cognitive processes are working okay. If this is in fact a roadblock, it had to have been placed here. If it were placed here, people did it. People mean what, though? Especially if they are the kind of people who make roadblocks and cause car crashes.

This cannot be the government, I decide. If it were, things would be more coordinated. The tractor-trailer trucks would all be identical, and there would be machine gun nests on top of them. I look up to ensure that I am right about the lack of machine gun nests. All I see are arrays of lights. But not vehicle lights; floodlights. Industrial-sized lighting used to illuminate the workspace on the highway when they have to do work at night. They are all pointed down into the box created by the bulldozers and trucks. It may not be government-organized, but it is organized.

I hear the door behind me creak open. Remembering my fragile brain, I turn slowly to look. It's Grace, and she is tumbling out the door onto the roadway. As quickly as I can, I go over and help her up. She's not steady, but she can stand okay. By the time she is oriented, Liam is in the doorway, ready to climb out. He does not appear any worse for the wear, but I'm sure that, like me, he is suffering from bruised ribs and a sore waistline from the seat belt.

Grace starts around the car to the passenger side and Liam and I follow. She goes right to the front door for Sofie. It's the first time I'm really looking at the front end. It is completely caved in and I can see Sofie's airbag through the window. Grace cannot open the door; the damage is too severe. But she won't give up, and she keeps pulling and straining.

The fact that Dad and Sofie may be dead highlights the damage in my skull. I cannot comprehend what that would mean. I cannot form a next step or an action plan. If Dad is gone, here—wherever we are—is the end of the road. We all die with him. I know I can't give up like this, but I also know that my brain is not functioning well enough to push on.

Grace starts pounding on the window. "Sofie! Wake up!" She's speaking loudly but not yelling. I don't know if there is a physical reason for her volume control or if she is worried about alerting someone to our presence. There is no way she could have identified the roadblock.

Liam is pushing Grace out of the way to get to the window. He has a rock in his hand and he is going to break the glass. As he pulls back to smash, Sofie's head rolls to the side and her eyes open. "Close your eyes and look the other way. We're going to get you out," Liam tells her calmly.

The glass breaks easily and Liam uses a shard to fully deflate the airbag. In what seems like one fluid motion, Sofie half-climbs, is half-pulled through the window and placed on the road. "I'm okay, I'm okay, I'm okay," she keeps repeating. She looks okay; I think her nose is broken, but, like the rest of us, she is struggling to get her thinking together.

After a few minutes on the ground, Sofie is up on her feet. She leans on Liam for support and starts surveying the scene. We haven't checked on Dad and no one has mentioned him either. It's odd. Sofie survived; why not him? I guess that we are so used to him being okay through everything he never needs to be checked on. In fact, I would bet that Grace and Liam assume he is out of the car and told me to take care of them while he looks for a new ride and a way out of this mess.

The four of us are standing together in silence behind the crumpled Escalade. My eyes have adjusted to the dark completely. I am reading the logos on the tractor-trailer cabs when a sudden blinding light sends me reeling. Grace and Sofie both spin into my chest and I instinctively put my arms around them. I can feel Liam beside me, leaning into our pile. In the background, I hear a generator running. That must be where the power for the lights is coming from.

After standing motionless for a few minutes, I want to check on Dad. But I am worried what will happen. The lights were not motion-activated; there was way too long of a delay for that. Someone turned them on. Strangely, I am not worried about what would happen to me. I'm worried for the others if I make a sudden move or give the appearance of trying to escape. I've never put others' well being ahead of my own. Is it Sofie or am I just maturing?

In front of us we hear a shuffling sound that is not labored but certainly not energetic or agile. Perhaps whoever set this roadblock was asleep and we have woken them with our crash. There is definitely more than one person there, but I can't tell if it is two, three or more. A click that I have only heard two or three times before raises the hair on the back of my neck. Our hosts have chambered a round in their shotgun.

When the two figures come into view, I am almost relieved at their frailty. Even I could take them in a fair fight. But this isn't a fair fight. They have guns and we don't. To make matters worse, they look drunk, or high, or a combination of the two. Wouldn't it be ironic if crystal meth were the cure for the "killer cold." I don't think I could do that to my body or my brain even if the alternative were death.

"Woohoo, they got girls for us!" shouts the man on my left. He's not a farmer or a laborer of any kind. "Hillbilly" is the only description that comes to mind.

The one on the right must be the brains of the operation. He is standing a little more upright and appears to have one tooth more than his friend.

"Where you all goin' in such a hurry?" The leader is speaking to me like I am somehow in charge. "We don't take kindly to people driving on our highway without permission." He gets it out just before a small coughing fit.

"We were headed to California." I want to add "before you two idiots almost killed us," but I hold my tongue. He has the "killer cold" and will be dead within 36 hours, but that shotgun of his can wreak havoc on us before he goes.

"Well, I guess some of you ain't gonna make it," he says with a demented chuckle. "The ladies can come over here with us," is coughed out while he raises the shotgun to his shoulder and aims carefully at my head. His partner is equally trained on Liam.

I never thought about whether you would hear the gun that shot you. I guess you do, though, because I clearly heard the two shots ring out. They were separate and distinct. Perhaps my shooter had a coughing fit that delayed him. Or his friend didn't know they were killing us and needed a second to catch up.

The pain hasn't set in yet, but somehow the hillbillies are slumping to the ground and I am still standing. There is complete silence. The girls aren't screaming; there are no orders coming from anywhere. We are just standing in the middle of the road, frozen in total shock. The bodies of our would-be killers are a pathetic lump of dirty clothes and stink.

In my head, I can remember the mist of blood that filled

the air but I don't remember actually seeing their heads explode. I once read about the physics involved with a head exploding due to a gunshot, but I can't think of the formulas for describing the event I just witnessed. There is no question the men are dead and their bodies do not need to be inspected. There is no action for us to take. We stand like statues.

"Everyone okay?" the voice from behind us is Dad's.

CHAPTER 18

We've been walking for about an hour and the sun is climbing higher in the sky. Before we rolled out this morning, I estimated about twenty miles of visibility from the top of the tractor-trailer truck we spent the restless night on. In those twenty miles there was nothing, just vast emptiness.

In addition to the scenic expanse, there was a completely gruesome sight. In the center median was a pile. At first glance, it looked like a pile of old clothes. I thought maybe someone had the idea to burn clothes of infected people to stop the spread of the virus. Unfortunately, the pile was made up of corpses. Virtually all of them were in uniform. Dad guessed it was National Guard. The sickening logistics of it all came to me while I stared. The pile was directly opposite one of the bulldozers. They must have backed trucks into the box, unloaded the bodies and then bulldozed them to the median. Then the truck got added to the roadblock.

As Grace and Liam assembled breakfast, Dad and I inspected every vehicle in the roadblock. All of them had their batteries removed. The missing batteries were nowhere to be found. It seems like a very intelligent way to disable a car without causing permanent damage. In the last truck on the western side of the roadblock, we found some of our answers.

A uniformed man with the clusters of a major sat in the cab of the truck with a laptop on the seat next to him. It had gone into sleep mode and still had 25 percent battery power. Knowing the military was here makes more sense than thinking those disgusting men put this together.

On the computer desktop was an .avi file. Dad told me to play it and I was expecting him to ask me to step away, but he didn't. The major's face filled the screen, and it was clear he was near death. Very little color in his face and a constant cough made the "killer cold" easy to diagnose.

The uniformed bodies were not from the National Guard; they were regular army, part of a medical detachment. The major noted with regret that they had started a massive fire just east of the Mississippi river in the hopes that they could destroy the contagion and protect the western half of the continent. After setting the fire, there had been some traffic on the freeway, so he and his team had decided to set up the roadblock to inspect people before letting them through. Sick people were turned away; some were denied passage with force. No healthy people had approached the roadblock.

His final comment was appropriately eerie. "I have not heard from central command in over a week. The few remaining members of my team have been sent west to rally in San Francisco. God help anyone who survives this."

While we walk, my thoughts take me back to those men that Dad murdered. I know it's not a fair assessment of his actions, but it is the term that keeps coming back to me. Yes, they had guns trained on his children. Yes, they were trying to take his daughter. Yes, they looked and sounded like they were under the influence of something. But where was the diplomacy? Where was the conversation? Is he just going to kill everyone we have a conflict with from now on?

My expectations of him are so high. It seems perfectly plausible to me that my Dad would have survived a 70 mile-per-hour head-on collision, silently exited the car and surveyed the area, then, upon seeing his children under the barrel of a gun, made his way around the assailants and disarmed them without a shot being fired. Once disarmed, he would have had a conversation with them about their actions, they would have apologized, and we would have two more people in our motley crew.

Perhaps my brain is more damaged than I realized.

I know that the average walking speed for a human is three miles per hour. If there is nothing for twenty miles, and we can maintain the average speed, we have a minimum of six hours of walking today, though we are likely in for a bigger chunk of the day than that. We are all sore from the crash, and between the fear that others would show up and the discomfort of sleeping outdoors on top of a tractor-trailer truck, it will be hard to average three miles per hour.

I find it odd that a medical team from the Army would carry the stop sticks that were laid across the highway, but again, I don't know much about military tactics. Perhaps the sticks were improvised and came from a police vehicle. But there was no police vehicle on-site and no indication of other law enforcement resources. So how did they get there?

It is frighteningly possible that the next town we come to will have people in it. Maybe the local law enforcement or even a militia group thought that they could quarantine themselves. They might have added the stop sticks for good measure and retreated to their town. Any guards for a quarantined town likely have orders to shoot to kill. That means we would get the same amount of conversation Dad gave to the two men back there: none. We had better stay alert.

"You guys better get used to walking," Dad says out of the blue. "I'm not sure how long it'll be before we get back to civilization."

"Can't we ride a bike?" Liam asks.

"Sure Liam, you can ride a bike," Dad says curtly.

I'm not sure why Dad's mad at Liam. He has a really good point. Bikes are a great form of transportation. They go faster and require less energy than walking.

"Um, Dad? Liam's got a really good point." I'm sticking up for my brother in what is effectively a useless argument.

There are no bikes around.

"Of course, he does Seamus. Why don't you hop on the next bike you see and ride off?" comes frustrated reply.

Liam is referencing the future and thinking about who knows what. Dad is thinking about the present but referencing the future. They are having two different conversations.

It's clear that Dad is on edge. I wonder if he is worried that there are guard posts with shoot-on-sight orders. Perhaps his tactical brain has come up with other, more likely scenarios that will result in our capture or death. Maybe he is injured more than any of us and is trying not to show it. Or maybe killing those two men last night is eating him up inside. I wish he would talk to us.

But this is how Dad works. He never brings things up himself. He always waits for us to bring it up. I wonder why he does this. Is it some sort of parenting trick? Like if he waits for us to bring something up, that's how he knows we are ready to discuss it and will listen to what he has to say? I guess you develop this approach through experience, but I really wish he would initiate a conversation for once.

Maybe thinking about stuff like this means I'm growing up. If I'm growing up, I guess I have to start some conversations, too. If I sincerely believe that we would all benefit from talking about last night, I had better start talking.

"Dad, are those the first people you've killed?" That didn't come out right.

Dead stop. Dad is staring at me in puzzlement. "Seriously, Seamus?"

"That didn't come out the way I wanted it to." I'm defensive, apologetic and a little scared.

"You've known me your whole life. Have I ever acted like someone who was comfortable with killing?" He's more disappointed than angry.

"Can we walk while we talk?" Sofie is unsure of how much she can push, but she's right, we need to keep moving.

"Do you somehow think that I enjoyed doing that last night? Do you think that I wanted to kill those men?" Dad is walking slightly ahead of the rest of us.

"No," we all murmur. But it seemed so easy from where we were standing. Everything seemed to happen so fast that there couldn't have been much deliberation or thought.

"Look, those men were both coughing. We all know that they would have died in the next day or two anyway. Why should I have let them put us all in danger of dying just so they could do drugs for another night?" Dad has a pretty clear justification for his actions.

"We know you're right," Grace chimes in. "It's just weird. Two weeks ago we got upset when someone posted a mean comment online. Now we can kill someone for threatening us?"

"How did we get here!?" Sofie is looking at the sky and screaming. "This is insane. I want to wake up from this nightmare. I want it all to be over."

"I want it to be over too Sofie. The truth is, I feel terrible. I know it was warranted. I know those men would have died soon anyway. But who gave me the right, the power to make the decision I made?" His voice is hoarse and deeply emotional. "I don't know how we got here or the best way for us to move on. I just know that we have to keep moving. We have to get to California. I hope none of us has to make another life-or-death decision. If that time does come again, I hope whoever it is has the strength to do the right thing for our family. Even if it will eat you up inside for the rest of your life."

We have each been given a license to kill. Family-first is the deciding factor in all future conflicts. It is unsettling, but not as much as the thought that it is necessary and likely to be in play more than once in the coming years.

After some more walking in silence, we come to a road sign. Cheyenne, Wyoming, is twelve miles away. The next exit is four miles. At this point we have been on the move for almost six hours. Two more hours, and we will be able to sit down and eat, get a drink and rest.

"When we get to California, I think I'm going to head out

on my own." Sofie is sharing her inner monologue. "I'd like to find a cottage on the beach where I can garden, and surf cast and live out my days reading classic novels."

"That sounds really beautiful. Can I come visit?" Grace is happy to venture off into fantasyland.

"It does sound nice, but that might not be the safest approach to surviving the near future." Dad wants us to make it through today.

"I know, but I don't think I'm cut out for rebuilding humanity or whatever the big picture is after we settle down." She seems comfortable with her decision and is not sharing so that we can change her mind.

"Well, after the mess we've made of this cross-country trip, I don't think any of us would have been nominated to rebuild humanity." Liam is dead serious, but his comment is hysterical.

After a good laugh that relaxes us all, Dad has the final word on the topic. "No one will force you to do anything, Sofie. I hope that for all of our sakes you will at least give us some time in California to figure out what the future might hold."

CHAPTER 19

After ten hours of walking, it is quite possible that we are having hallucinations. On the rickety old swing set behind the truck stop, there is a little kid swinging, as if it were the most normal thing in the world. He is not alarmed by our presence and, in fact, doesn't even seem to notice us.

Sadly, Dad has gripped his gun and made sure that there is a round in the chamber. Surely he can't see this little person as a threat. Grace isn't even aware of Dad's actions; she wants to go help the child.

"Grace" is all Dad says to stop her. He then leads us over behind a storage container and puts his backpack down.

This is ridiculous. I'm about to speak my mind when Dad puts a finger to his lips.

"If this is a trap, I want you all to run. Sofie and Seamus, pair up and stay together; Grace and Liam, pair up and stay together." He's whispering but is crystal clear. "Pairs should spread out. If we have to escape, meet up at the next mile marker down the highway. If we are not all there by daybreak, head out and keep going west."

Whoa, a trap. "Do you really think a four-year-old is going to set a trap for us?"

"No, but he is the perfect bait." Dad is anxiously looking

around. "This is the first civilization since the roadblock. We have to assume they could be involved with that setup out on the highway."

This is what Sofie was talking about, fear of every human encounter. Even a four-year-old results in a drawn weapon and worst-case scenario plan. I don't think I'm cut out for this either. I wonder if Sofie will let me share her cottage by the sea.

"Sofie and Seamus, you stay here. Grace and Liam, you make your way around the building and meet me at the swing set." He's planning more of an assault than a rescue.

Sofie and I watch silently as Dad cautiously walks across the parking lot towards the swing set. Liam is doing his best impersonation of a commando and Grace is just walking quickly while fishing for something in her pocket.

Sofie is fighting an urge to charge out and join them. She pushes against me as if relying on my body for restraint. I want to tell her that Dad is a good man; he is not the one injecting fear and hostility into the world. He has every right to be cautious and we need to appreciate the fact that he's looking out for all of us.

When his feet touch the wood chips surrounding the swing set, Dad's gun moves from his hand to the back waistband of his jeans. This is Sofie's cue, and she sprints off across the parking lot. It is all I can do to keep up with her—stopping her is not an option. Liam and Grace also close in on the swing set. We will be there momentarily.

I'm the last one to arrive, but I get there in time to hear the boy speak. "I'm from Colorado."

"Wow, Colorado. That's a cool state." Dad is getting down on a knee so he is at eye level with the little boy. "Is your Mom or Dad around?"

"I'm three," is his response. It takes a few seconds but he manages to get three fingers in the air to show us his age.

"Three! I knew you were a big boy." Dad has a way with little kids. "We would really like to meet your Mom or Dad and let them know how good you are behaving."

"They're sleepin'," he says, while looking around as if he may point to where it is they are sleeping.

"Oh, did they lay down for a nap while you came to swing?" Dad is not afraid, but there is apprehension in his voice. Helping a three-year-old realize that his parents are dead may prove more emotional than what he had to do last night.

"I don't know. They been sleepin' a long time." The boy is nodding his head as if to confirm his statement. "Can I have a snack?"

"Sure, I have one right here." Grace has a granola bar at the ready. That must be what she had been fishing out of her pocket. She's kneeling by the swing next to Dad and opening the snack for the little guy. Grace is a natural.

"What's your name, buddy?" Liam can't stay out of it. At least it's a good question.

"I'm from Colorado," is the reply between bites. Maybe that was the first thing Dad had asked him, and he doesn't know or has chosen to forget his name.

So we have a nameless 3-year-old survivor from Colorado. A leftover. The only remaining artifact from an unknown family. A remnant. "Is it okay if we call you Remmie?" I ask him. "Everyone needs to have a name."

Dad, Grace and Sofie look at me like I have two heads.

Grace stands up with her arms out. "Come on buddy, let's go into this store and see if we can find a drink and a bigger snack." Her glare lets me know that I should keep my mouth shut, but I'm not sure why.

He goes to her arms easily and they head off towards the store. You can see from the little boy's face that it has been a while since he has eaten. Liam falls in close behind. We could all use a drink and something to eat, but Sofie and Dad are hanging back with me. I may be in for a lecture.

"You can't just rename a 3-year-old." Dad is acting like I just set the world back to the dark ages.

"Seriously, Seamus. Give the little kid a break. He's malnourished, dehydrated and his parents just died. It's okay if he needs some time before he can tell us his name." Sofie is

126

not impressed with me right now. Probably not a good time to ask about sharing her cottage on the beach.

"For now, why don't we stick with calling him 'buddy,'" Dad says as he heads back towards the storage trailer. "If he doesn't tell us and we don't find any clues about his name, we can decide what to call him then."

Sofie is heading off towards the store and shaking her head. All I can do is sit down in the swing and wonder what I did so wrong. He's not going to tell us his name. I don't remember being three but I do remember when my cousins were that age. It was hit or miss getting their names out of them, a 50/50 chance at best. I'll bet that if they didn't hear them for two days they would have forgotten them completely.

I guess I have always tried to shortcut social norms. But we are in a new post-apocalyptic world; social norms need to go out the window. We need to be able to cut to the chase and move on. We can't spend energy and resources culling names out of little kids.

Boy, do I sound like a hardass. Maybe this is another thing Sofie was talking about not wanting to be a part of.

"Seamus! Come in here and get something to eat and drink." Liam is yelling from the side of the store. He is not struggling with the impact of rebuilding society.

Inside the store, there are hot dogs on rollers, popcorn and chips, coolers full of any beverage you could want. Grace and Remmie (I'm still calling him Remmie, no matter what they say) are sitting in a booth eating hot dogs and drinking chocolate milk. I can see that he has some goldfish crackers on his plate and she has a cup of peaches nearby that she'll probably get him to eat against his will.

Liam is walking around eating from a bag of chips and searching after the open drink he put down but now cannot find. Sofie has her head tilted back with a bottle of water. On the counter in front of her is an unopened box of Pop tarts. I didn't realize how hungry I was until now. There has to be something I can microwave and then stuff into my face. I grab a water as I look through the coolers for something edible.

Dad comes out of the bathroom and surveys the scene. He's got a wry smile on his face and seems more than satisfied with where we've ended up for the day. He walks to the cooler and grabs a water before he starts to peruse the aisle for his meal.

"After I eat a little I'm going to go out and find a car." Dad is not addressing anyone of us in particular. "Grace and Sofie, will you keep an eye on our little friend?" His question is met with nods of their heads. "Liam and Seamus, I want you to find some bedding. I think we should sleep here tonight, but I don't want to wake up feeling the way I did this morning," he says with his hand on his back.

We all just came through the same parking lot, so I know it is going to be a frustrating exercise for him. I remember seeing a few tractor-trailer rigs, a beat up old Mustang, and a pickup with no bed. None of these will get the six of us down the road together, and I know he won't want us to split up even if we could travel in caravan formation.

Dad is out the door with his water and a bagel and Liam pats me on the back. He's pointing to the sign on the wall that says "Showers and Suites" with an arrow pointing to the back of the building. I never thought about it, but it makes sense that truck stops have places for drivers to crash for a few hours and freshen up.

When we see the accommodations, "cell" seems a far more appropriate description. The "suite" is a six-foot by six-foot cube with a short bed and a tiny stall shower. An efficiency expert or designer who would never have to spend a night here was paid handsomely to lay out this space. I'm glad we won't have to close ourselves into one of these for the night. There are eight units in total and Liam and I grab the bedding from four of them. A few extra pillows and blankets won't hurt.

As we get back to the main part of the building, I can see a cargo van pull up to the pumps. Dad hops out and walks around to fill it up. I guess we are all being relegated to cargo status. This is a far cry from the two Cadillac Escalades we have enjoyed up to this point in our trip.

CHAPTER 20

It seemed only fitting that we had to go backwards to move forward. We went back to the roadblock and the crashed Escalade to get our things. I can't believe I had completely forgotten about my lab equipment. Fortunately even a cargo van makes the 22-mile trip fast. Dad and I made the trip alone while Liam searches for confirmation of Remmie's parents and possibly his name. Grace and Sofie are organizing supplies while the kid sleeps.

On both of the Escalades we have used to date, the Thule roof top carriers were properly mounted according to the directions. On this cargo van, they are tied through open windows and sliding around a bit on the roof. After the fire and the crash, I'm not too worried about my stuff anymore. The guns and our personal effects fit easily. It's not called a cargo van for nothing and there is a lot more room in here than we had previously. Seating is an issue, but there is no one to pull us over for violating the seat belt laws.

By the time we get back to the truck stop, the rest of the gang is on the swing set waiting. We are all moving mechanically as we load the food supplies into the van. There is no spring in anyone's step. While there is no desire to spend another night here, getting on the highway and racing down the road seems to have no allure either.

"Um, I found them." Liam actually looks like he wants to cry. "They had a picture of him. I looked at the back but it didn't have his name. I checked for a wallet or a purse or something, but no dice. The safe was closed so maybe they were in there." Tears are streaming down his face, but his voice is steady.

Dad walks over and puts an arm around him. "I know that was hard. I'm sorry you had to experience that."

Until now we have been spared looking at dead bodies. Dad has done all the gruesome work of checking places before we enter. I thought it was a safety check. Now I realize that he was relocating corpses. But Liam has taken a huge step. Dad trusted him with an important task and let him feel sadness, discomfort and emotional pain. Sophie, Grace, and I have still been spared the dead bodies; it's Dad and Liam that will have those memories. It has me rethinking the roster of the grown-up team.

"So we are just going to take him?" Sofie is questioning our next move.

I don't see how there can be any question. We are not going to stay here forever. We are not going to leave a 3-year-old alone. Yes, of course we are going to take him.

"Well Sofie, Wyoming is a far cry from the beach. There is no surfcasting here and that garden of yours may not have many productive months." Dad is somewhere between lecture and concession speech. "Are you proposing that the two of you stay here, alone, together?"

Wait, this can't be happening. There is no way we are leaving Sofie alone in Hillsdale, Wyoming. What can I say that doesn't sound desperate, that makes sense, and convinces her that they have to come with us?

"No. Of course I'm not suggesting that," Sofie says with a confused look on her face. "I just feel like we should say something. Give him the token chance to say what he wants to do. Because..." She trails off and looks at the floor.

"Because we never gave Sofie the choice of coming with

us or not," Grace finishes the thought. "We assumed that she would be better off with us. In some respects, we took advantage of her when she was in a state of shock from losing her parents."

"It sounds awful when you say it out loud like that!" Sofie is horrified that this is what she was thinking. "I am better off with all of you. I am grateful for you everyday. It just feels like it wasn't by choice. Even if it's pretend, let's give Remmie a choice."

"You know what?" Dad looks ready to lay into all of us. His voice is raised and Mr. Nice Guy is nowhere around.

I can imagine what he is about to say and he is right. Things are different now. You're not always going to get to make a choice. Not everyone has a say in what happens. Choices are binary; you come with us and live, or you stay behind and die. Make the decision; don't stand around talking about it. When we get to California, you can act like an independent, selfish adult. Then when you're starving and thirsty come find us again and we'll take you back in.

A long exhale from Dad precedes his statement: "Fine. Give him the choice and then mount up. We need to get moving and get a new car."

Of course he agreed to come with us. He also agreed to answer to Remmie. The name thing makes it feel weirdly like abduction. No one offered him candy to come with us, but I am creeped out by the outside view of what just happened. *"Hey little boy, get in our van and come with us. Let's pretend your name is Remmie and you're going on an adventure."* It's the right thing, but I hope our approach doesn't scar him for life.

On the road I can see that Dad is not just being vain about getting a new car. The transmission in the van keeps slipping and the tires are way out of balance. There is no way this vehicle can sustain speed and get over the mountains safely. We thump along in silence, knowing that there will be another stop before we get going again.

It's only three exits before we see the sign for a Chevy dealership. I'm hoping that a Suburban will be our fourth and final transport for the trip. Dad heads into the dealership to get keys while the rest of us unload the cargo van. We are silent and efficient. I can't speak for the others, but I just want the task to be over. Let's get in the car, head down the road and veg out.

As I untie my rooftop carriers, I wonder if I should look inside to check on my equipment. Do I want to know? If it's damaged or ruined there is nothing I can do about it. All that will happen is I'll be upset for a few hours and get angry about things that no one could have controlled. None of us need that. I'll leave them closed until we get to California.

With the rooftop carriers mounted properly and the equipment and food transferred to the back, we are ready to move out. "Seamus, why don't you sit up front with me?" Dad is looking at Remmie while he speaks.

I think that technically Remmie is supposed to be in a car seat, but we don't bother. If there is another epic car crash, he won't want to survive it. Plus with Grace's arm around him he has a look of contentment and innocence that we are all longing for. Right now, being physically close with a human is more important than traditional highway safety.

The mountains approach almost immediately. Though we have seen them coming since we walked away from the road block, it seems like they rise from nowhere. We have spent a lot of time in the White Mountains of New Hampshire, hiking, skiing and sightseeing, but they are nothing compared with the Rockies. It's hard to believe that they both get to be called mountains. It doesn't seem fair.

After a few hours of driving and watching the breathtaking scenery, I grab Dad's phone from the console. No bars. How long has it been since we spoke to Mom? I'm thinking it's been at least two days. We were supposed to have met up with her last night in San Francisco. She must be worried sick, and more than a little bit angry.

I suppose angry wouldn't be what she felt. That's me projecting. I'm angry that I forgot to check last night. Angry that I didn't pick up the landline and try her. In fact, I can't even remember thinking about her. No, Mom's not angry. I am.

"Thanks for trying, bud." Dad's glancing at me while trying to keep his eyes on the road. "I think our next conversation with Mom is going to be in person." He's trying to eek out a smile but it won't seem to come. "I checked last night. Heh, I even tried the landline to see if we could connect to anything."

I hope they built travel delays into their plans for meeting up. I wish they would have let me in on the plan or even let me orchestrate it. Dad misses so many details and contingency scenarios. It seems like he prefers going to Plan B most of the time.

As I think about contingencies, the first snowflake hits the window. "Seriously?" The word comes out of my mouth before I can even process what a snowflake might mean.

"It's snowing!" Grace hasn't processed what snow might do to us. "Look Remmie, it's snowing outside. Do you like to play in the snow?"

I want to give her a lecture about the problems snow can cause us. We are not on a ski trip and there is no school to be canceled tomorrow. Snow is cold and slippery and we are not prepared for it.

"Dad? What happens if they don't plow the roads when it snows?" Liam asks. He could piece this together if he would spend a minute thinking about his question before speaking. But not Liam, he would rather hear the noise of his own voice.

"Really Liam? What do you think is going to happen?" Dad normally has little patience for questioning the obvious; now he has none.

"The road will get covered and we can't drive?" Liam is answering as if there is a chance he is wrong. "I mean, did they ever not plow at home? Are we going to be able to keep going?" He has a concern in his head but he struggles to get it out.

"We are going to push on while we can. If it gets dangerous, I'll get off the highway and we can find a place to hunker down." Dad is part communicating, part convincing himself of a course of action.

Fortunately there is not a lot of accumulation. The snow is sticking on the grass but blows easily off the road. It seems to go on like this for hours and miles. Our top speed is down in the low 70s. It's feels borderline safe, but I'm sure Dad considers anything slower to be the same as stopped.

The sun is getting low and dark is approaching fast. We have already had a bad experience driving at night. Driving at night in the snow is a downright terrifying thought. I'm about to ask if we can pull over and find a place for the night when we see a billboard for the Hyatt at the Salt Lake City Airport.

"I can't believe it took us this long to get here," Dad says as he fiddles with the navigation display. "I was hoping we could make Nevada before nightfall."

The snow has stopped and Dad has us back up to 100 miles an hour. "I think we should stop at that Hyatt we just passed the sign for." It's my first act as co-pilot. "It's twenty miles away. We can be there in less than fifteen minutes."

"Agreed," he says as we both look to the navigation screen like it has an answer.

The map is still being displayed, but our vehicle location is not being modified. I can't believe that we got the Suburban with the defective navigation unit. I look closer only to realize that it stopped hours ago, while we were in the mountains. Dad must have realized this, which is why he was fiddling with it.

"I thought it was the snow causing problems," Dad looks at me while he speaks. "But now I think the satellites may be shutting down."

Of course. The satellite designers made accommodations for prolonged communications failures. If the satellite doesn't hear from earth for a few weeks, it shuts down and moves to a safer orbit.

"Good thing I-80 is a straight shot to San Francisco. Even I can't get lost," Dad says.

CHAPTER 21

What is it with the post-apocalypse and early mornings? If we get to San Francisco before four in the afternoon, I am going to let Dad know how bad his time planning is. There is no Internet and no landlines, so we are still in the dark as far as communicating with Mom.

Grace and Sofie shared a room with Remmie. That kid is a real trooper. He hasn't complained about anything and even tries to help without being asked. He also has a sense of humor and laughs at some pretty random stuff. Dad, Liam and I all had our own rooms with king-sized beds. The sleep was magnificent. If Mom was not waiting for us, I would be strongly pushing to spend another night here. If the past few days have taught me anything, it's that you never know what kind of mess you could wind up in on the road.

Just imagining Mom and her smile and her voice helped get me going, though. Getting that hug I know is waiting and sharing all the crazy things that Liam and Grace did on our trip will make me forget the pain we have endured. Last night, with a paper map and a ruler, Dad estimated that we have 900 miles to go before reaching San Francisco. After he went to bed I took the map and came up with closer to 700 miles. He is so imprecise it kills me.

Regardless of who made the better estimate, we have 7 to 9 hours of driving ahead of us today. That assumes that there will be no snow, no roadblocks and no other natural disasters. I'm riding shotgun again, and the girls were able to add some coloring books, board games and G-rated videos for Remmie. I'm hopeful for an event-free day, but I am not optimistic.

About an hour west of Salt Lake, we are in a serious mountain pass. The road conditions are fine but there are patches of snow underneath trees and in some shady spots. Fortunately the sky is clear and stunningly blue. Weather will not be a problem this morning. However, I do feel like I need to remain awake and vigilant. In the back of my mind, I recall the old stagecoaches and the origination of the term "shotgun." It is not a stretch to think that I should have a weapon readily available to me.

"Dad, do you think I should have a gun up here?" I ask him casually so as not to alarm the passengers.

He surveys the mountains around us as if there was something there. "I suppose that makes some sense." He pauses but I know there is more. "I don't think it's urgent though. Let's wait until our little friend is asleep. Then we can have one passed up."

Finding Nemo is still a big hit with little kids and even Liam seems to be enjoying it. They are snacking and laughing at the film. I am torn between wanting to be in the back watching movies with the kids and my pride for being up front in the true "shotgun" position. I look out the window, and my mind wanders to what we will need to get done once we arrive in San Francisco.

"Why don't you hold off on another movie for a bit? See if anyone wants to close their eyes and rest." Dad's voice interrupts my thinking. I'm not sure how long I was gone, but *Nemo* must be over.

My vigilance out the windows returns and, after about ten minutes, Dad whispers to the back: "Liam. Can you get one of the shotguns and a handful of shells and pass them up here to Seamus?"

When having a weapon was my idea, it felt logical and smart. When Dad puts it into action, it feels scary. Did he see something or someone? I suppose that as long as he leaves his handgun in the console I should feel safe. The barrel of the shotgun pokes me in the shoulder and I reach back to bring it forward. Guns are always heavier than I expect. Next come two handfuls of shells. Couldn't he have just sent up the box?

"Make sure you load it," Dad says, looking out the window.

Now I am frightened again. As calmly as I can, I load all of the shells into the shotgun. I'm gripping it tightly across my lap, wary of the trigger and keeping my finger well away from it.

"Now point the muzzle to the floor, and let go of the gun." Dad is talking in very soothing tones. He must sense my tension, "Seamus, there is nothing to be afraid of. We have clear sailing ahead."

Famous last words, I think to myself as I lower the gun and look out the side window. Before long, I am fast asleep. Even after last night's magnificent rest, I am in a deep slumber.

Eventually I begin to dream. Sofie and I are by the ocean. She is gardening and I am sitting on the deck of a small cottage reading a book. The sky is beautiful, the sun is warm on my face, and we are both so happy. But then commandos appear. Out of nowhere. They are rappelling down ropes from helicopters! Sofie is caught and is being forced face-down onto the ground. Now they've got me; I twist to get out of their grip, but it is too firm.

"Seamus, we're coming into Reno," I hear Dad's voice before I open my eyes. "We're making really good time today."

Like every other town and city we have passed through, Reno is quiet. I don't see any sign of life or electricity. I'm sure that the hydroelectric plants will fail eventually, but I didn't think it would happen this soon. Maybe it's more along the lines of a blown transformer or something breaking at the power substation.

"Are we going to stop for gas?" I ask, even though I can't

see the gauge.

"Yeah, there is a service area in a few miles. I thought we would gas up, stretch and get a little fresh air." Dad is nodding while he speaks. I agree that it's a good idea.

The service area has no power. From the state of the coolers, it has not been off for long; the drinks are still cold. We agree that any refrigerated food is off-limits and snack from the shelves with preservative-loaded foods. Dad is outside, working the manual pump rig. Once I get a drink and some Fritos, I'll go out and relieve him.

Dad and Liam wind up playing a little football while Remmie plays hide-and-seek with Grace and Sofie. I'm content to operate the manual pump and watch them relax. The stop takes a lot longer than I had anticipated, but it is event free. I wonder if I'm the only one who is suddenly nervous about meeting up with Mom?

After blowing through Sacramento like it wasn't there, we are on the San Francisco Bay Bridge. Off to my right, I catch a glimpse of the Golden Gate Bridge. It is a magnificent structure. Even though it is quite common and even rudimentary technology by today's standards, its brilliance is clear. I can see the water of the bay rushing below us. Not only designing but also building a structure that can stand up to the massive power of the ocean is a feat. Having done so in the early 1900s is beyond my comprehension.

With no phones and no navigation, I'm not sure how we are going to find Mom. Dad has a street name but not an address or directions. Did they assume that navigation would be working and it would be obvious where humans were? It's not like we can stop and ask someone for directions.

I'm combing through the paper map we picked up in Reno. I found the street name, but getting there from the highway is not straightforward. It seems like there are 100 turns we need to make over the course of less than a mile. The sun is getting low and I can't imagine we'll be able to find anything here in the dark.

We get off the highway and come to a stop. The tension in

the Suburban is thick. The streets are empty and we don't have to obey the stop sign we are in front of.

"I think you can go," Liam says from the back.

"I'm giving Seamus a minute to get his bearings and find out where we are on the map." Dad is looking in the rear view mirror addressing the back seat driver. "You kids aren't used to paper maps. You've always had navigation and touch screens. I'll wait while you adjust."

"I've got it! Up seven streets, left for three streets and then right for four more streets." I'm not even sure how to read out directions off of the paper map.

"Okay," he chuckles. "Remmie, can you help the big kids count streets?"

After we start moving again I blurt out, "You're looking for a left on 20th Street." This feels like the right way to navigate for a driver. I think I remember he and Mom doing this when I was little.

Dad keeps slowing down as we approach stop signs. I want him to just blow through them. There is no one here and we are almost to Mom. Keep your foot on it, old man.

After we make the left, it's as if he has heard my thoughts. The stop signs are whizzing by in a blur. We go three streets in the blink of an eye. The hard right has us all feeling as many G-forces as a Suburban can manage. I think we are back to our 100 mph average. If Mom is waiting in the street for us, we won't be able to stop.

Dad doesn't start to apply the brakes until after we pass the fourth street. It's not obvious to me where Mom is staying, but maybe Dad can sense her presence? Now he's hanging a U-turn and moving much more slowly. He pulls to the first cross street and stops, looking up and down the road. I do not want to spend a night in San Francisco without finding Mom.

We slowly roll to the next cross street and, there on the corner, in the last bit of sunshine on the street, is Mom. She is standing defiantly with her hands on her hips. Her face possesses not quite a scowl but certainly not the smile I was expecting.

We don't know quite what to do. Why aren't we bursting out of the truck and running to her? There should be smiles and laughter and cheering. We made it!

Dad slams the SUV into park and Grace starts the eruption. Her door flies open and her cry of "Mom!" fills the vehicle. Mom's face breaks into a broad smile and she is running the short distance to the car while I get my door open. I manage to make up the small gap between Grace and me so that we meet in Mom's embrace at almost the exact same moment. An instant later, Liam is on us completing our group hug and adding to the "I love you's," tears and laughter bubbling out of our pile.

When we finally break our embrace, I see Dad holding Sofie. From the heaving of her back I can tell that she is sobbing. There is no reunion coming for her. Seeing us with Mom and realizing that our family is reunited is a painful reminder of what she has lost.

Grace hurries over to console her and Dad takes the opportunity to greet Mom. They hug tightly and then share a long kiss. The stress is completely gone from Dad's face and posture. We are all back together. Whatever happens from here out doesn't matter. I doubt that we will ever separate for long again.

"You're late," are the first real words out of her mouth. But she's not mad. "I'm so glad you are all okay, I have been so worried I don't think I've slept in two weeks." She's standing and surveying all of us like we're being inspected before the first day of school.

"Come inside! We were just wondering if we should hold dinner for a third straight night." She's turned and is walking toward the steps of the closest house.

CHAPTER 22

The house we've entered is like a museum, but comfortable. Strangely, it does not feel like we are squatters here. There are still family pictures up and personal effects lying around. The "we" Mom mentioned are the homeowners. She is their guest.

Whoever they are, the smell in the house matches the décor: elegant. While Grace and Sofie have kept us fed, the circumstances have not been conducive to real cooking. Here we have encountered a gourmet *tour de force*. If the food being prepared tastes as good as it smells, I may eat for days.

Mom walks through a door and holds it open. I enter the kitchen and am immediately struck by the warmth. My eyes scan the faces of the two women standing there. They are the two women from the family photos, a mother and her daughter is my guess. The difference from the pictures is that the younger woman looks slightly older and far more attractive than her pictures portrayed.

"Seamus! It's so good to see you," the mother is crossing from the stove to greet me. She embraces me in a stiff uncomfortable hug. The others are delayed from getting into the kitchen because of where she has stopped me.

I move further into the kitchen and awkwardly say "hello," to the daughter.

As Grace and Liam come through the door, the mother's smile remains but the enthusiasm of her greeting has come down a level. "You must be Grace and Liam," she clumsily pats them on the back. "And this must be Paddrick." She formally extends a hand as Dad walks in, but then allows her smile to fade.

The welcome portion of our arrival seems to be wrapping up. I find it odd that she said "nice to see you" and not "nice to meet you." While she clearly knows who we are, there was no declaration of how much Mom has told her about us. Things feel icky but I'm not sure why.

When Dad turns to bring Sofie and Remmie into the room, you would think he was introducing a pet lion. The mother's face goes white with shock. "

Who is this?" spews from her mouth. My family and I were not just expected: we were anticipated. Sofie and Remmie don't fit her plan.

"I would like to introduce Ms. Sofie Lange and Mr. Remmie Colorado," Dad says, trying to lighten the mood and spare Sofie the embarrassment of having survived the plague that killed billions. "Sofie has been with us since New Hampshire, and Remmie joined us a couple of days ago in Wyoming."

Both mother and daughter are in shock and not moving. I'm wondering if they are really considering ostracizing two of the last nine people on the planet. Fortunately Remmie breaks the tension.

"I'm three!" he says, getting those three little fingers in the air.

"Well, aren't you the big boy." My Mom bends over and wiggles his fingers in a way that makes him giggle.

Grace reaches down and scoops him up. "We are so proud of Remmie! He's such a big boy and really good at riding in the car."

"Let me introduce you to our hosts." Mom is trying to avoid silence. "This is Jane and Cassandra Crenshaw. They have lived in this beautiful home for the last ten years and now they are sharing it with us."

"Enough formality, you must be starving. Let's sit down and eat." Cassandra has adapted faster than her mother. "I'll just grab two more place settings for Sofie and Remmie. We can squeeze them in around Grace."

I get why they wouldn't be prepared for Remmie. We haven't spoken to Mom since we found him. But Sofie has been with us since home. Mom knew about her; they had to have known there were at least five of us coming. I'm wondering if Jane and Cassandra are the only other people in this house.

Grace is carrying on about a piece of art she saw on the way in. Liam is telling Mom that we saw snow yesterday and the tension level is down, but not gone. Sofie is sitting between Grace and Dad while Remmie is on the other side of Grace, next to Liam. I'm between Dad and Cassandra in a way that feels very orchestrated.

"I'm sorry that the lamb was frozen, it was the best we could do. But the vegetables are fresh and your Mom said this is how you like your rice." Jane is in hostess mode and, while it seems genuine, I have my doubts.

The food is exquisite. Any reservations I have about these people can wait. I need to get more into my mouth. I'm sure that we look like starved and disgusting animals, but for tonight, at least, we are given a pass on table manners. I need to take a break from eating, but not before I enjoy another piece of bread.

As I sit back to digest, Cassandra turns slightly. "So you're into physics? How is your work coming?"

While I admit to not being the most socially savvy, this seems like a strange way to phrase her question. She should be asking me what types of things I'm working on or what I'm interested in. Her tone and word choice make it seem like she knows things I haven't told her.

I guess the contorted look on my face gives away my confusion. Mom jumps in. "Seamus, Jane is a theoretical physicist at the NASA Ames Research Center. Cassandra is an experimental physicist with advanced degrees in mathematics and artificial intelligence. They work together on some very interesting technologies."

Being physicists and, in Cassandra's case, having a super intellect explains a great deal of the odd behavior.

"I graduated from Cal Poly with a PhD. in physics at sixteen. I've spent the three years since working with my mother at Ames and getting my additional degrees." Cassandra says with pride. I can tell she has been told her whole life that she is wonderful because she's brilliant.

I want to give my Dad a hug for not letting me graduate early and become like Cassandra. Being brilliant does not make you wonderful. These are not great people because of their brains, fine artwork and creases in the napkins. They may be nice and even kind, but short of feeding us I have seen no evidence as such.

"So you both work for the government?" Sofie has placed her fork and napkin on her plate. The comment is met with an odd chain reaction of Dad putting his hand gently on her thigh, Mom staring at Dad open-jawed, and Sofie glowering at both Jane and Cassandra.

If everyone were armed, I think that there would be guns drawn. Sofie's implication resonates with me immediately. It took a few seconds longer for Dad but he got there. Grace and Liam defer to our side of the argument without really knowing what it is.

They work for the government. They know me and my family and the power reactor technology I am working on. They survived the virus and assumed I would, too. They had to have been involved in all of it. There is no movement or speech. Assumptions are being made and conclusions being drawn. Dad looks ready to push back from the table and walk out of the house.

"I'm sorry, this is my fault." Mom has regained her voice. "I should have communicated better. I should have understood what you all had been through before just assuming you'd be ready to sit down to a formal dinner."

There is no way Mom was involved in this, is there? She hated election time because of all the signs, stupid ads and polling calls. How could she have worked for the government? It doesn't make any sense.

"We're all exhausted and emotionally drained. This has been quite a day." Mom is an accomplished business executive and she knows how to control a room. "Why don't we all get a good night's sleep? We can get all our questions out and answered tomorrow over brunch."

"Mom," Liam pauses after he starts. "We're not on vacation. I don't know what's going to happen tomorrow, but I'd be willing to bet we can't afford to wait until after *brunch* to get started."

Her veneer cracks and Mom gets up and leaves the room. On her way out, I can see a tear on her face. Through the door I hear a muffled cry and then she's gone. Liam was not trying to be mean or hurt her. He's right though. We don't know if they have enough provisions for us here. We have no idea what the area is like and how we would defend it if we had to. It doesn't seem like a good place for a permanent base; we should start looking for better places to settle down. Mom's experience tells her this place is safe. Our experience tells us you need to always be prepared for the worst.

I feel like I should get up and follow her. I'm a little surprised that Dad didn't run after her. They were always a pretty tight team before this. I should probably take my cue from him, but then again I should be my own person. I look to Grace to see if she has any guidance, but she's occupied with Remmie.

Sofie stands slowly. "Thank you for dinner. These days food is becoming a precious commodity. Sharing some of yours with us means a lot. Can I help clean up in the kitchen?" She's gracious and strong in the face of doubt and confusion. This is what makes a person wonderful.

"You are very welcome. And please leave the cleanup to us. We are happy to do it." Jane's voice is measured and her eyes are searching. She wants to find a common ground, but where? "We've made up rooms. Cassandra will show you upstairs and get you settled."

Cassandra rises and Sofie turns to leave. As they reach the doorway, Jane speaks again. "It may not help, but we lost loved ones, too. My parents, my sister, my niece and nephew." Her eyes are red and puffy; she is not the callous warmonger I projected onto her.

"My dad," Cassandra speaks and stares blankly at the floor. We've all experienced loss and it affects us in strange ways. My anger and hatred are fading, but trust is kept in reserve.

"Goodnight," Jane says quietly, and disappears into the kitchen.

The rest of us follow Cassandra up to the second floor. There are five bedrooms and a big linen closet. One room each for Cassandra and Jane, and one for Mom and Dad, leaves two bedrooms. Liam takes the first empty one, and Grace puts her arm around Sofie and they walk into the next one with Remmie toddling behind. I'm okay crashing with Liam, but I want to see if Dad goes in to talk with Mom. Having them torn apart is not an option.

As I lurk in the doorway, I hear him ask Cassandra, "Is it okay if I go downstairs and have a nightcap?" They'll have to sort things out in their own time. They always do.

CHAPTER 23

When I arrived in the kitchen this morning, I was not surprised to find Grace and Sofie sitting at the table sipping coffee. They greeted me sweetly and then resumed their conversation about things to do in San Francisco. Clearly the two of them are refreshed and not the least bit concerned about the results of our impending conversation.

Soon after I poured my coffee, Cassandra arrived in the kitchen. She was dressed for work, in high heels a knee-length skirt and a white silk blouse. I can't help but smile and think that if you added glasses and a lab coat, she would be the proverbial "sexy scientist." While I am able to keep the thought to myself, she does not share my smile or the positive energy in the room.

"Oh. Good morning," she says stiffly. "Coffee is typically reserved for the commute to Ames."

"If it's out, I can make more." Grace is standing and ready to walk over to the coffee maker.

"No. It appears that there is plenty left." Cassandra is filling her travel mug.

"Are there other people down at this Ames place?" Sofie swirls the coffee in her mug.

"My mother would like to be present for any

conversations about Ames." Cassandra's face is blank and gives no hints to the answer.

"Seriously?" Sofie places her cup on the table. "There are nine people left on the planet and you and your mom want to keep secrets?"

"I did not achieve top0secret clearance at a NASA research center because I play fast and loose with information." Cassandra is a little angry that we are questioning her. "You will get appropriate answers to all your questions when my mother is ready. She will be down shortly."

She turns to leave the room, but is interrupted with another question, this time from Grace. "So are you just going to go to work as usual?"

"Right now I'm going to the dining room." She is not up for conversation.

"Seamus, I would say she seems like your type, if she wasn't such a bitch." Sofie is smiling and Grace giggles along with the joke.

How did we arrive at this "us vs. them" mentality? We cannot afford to be fighting with anyone. So they worked for the government. It seems like something fishy has left us all as survivors. But we are survivors, and none of us can keep going on our own.

Dad comes into the kitchen. He looks like hell. He probably wound up having more than one nightcap.

"You guys wanna come into the dining room?" He's a little hoarse, which fits how he looks. "Jane just got down and she's ready to answer some questions."

We file into the dining room and Cassandra and her mom are sitting together on one side of the table. Mom is not in the room, and I have no idea how this is supposed to work. This is not a trial; we are not enemies.

Jane breaks the ice. "Let me start with an apology. From the time that Cassandra was twelve, she has been a target."

Um, this is not how I expected things to go.

"What kind of target?" Sofie is in hardball mode.

"Mostly kidnapping, probably assassination." Jane is very

academic about her daughter's life. "From what the FBI and CIA told us, the Chinese and the North Koreans believed that if they kidnapped her at a young enough age, they could brainwash her into working for them. There was also more than one global defense contractor who thought a boyfriend or girlfriend could get information out of her. It is amazing what adults will do to try and manipulate a 15-year-old girl."

"And you think Seamus and his family are okay, but not Remmie or me?" Sofie wants to get all the angles out on the table.

Mom quietly slips into the room and stands at the end of the table. She has literally not chosen a side.

"No." Jane remains emotionless. "I want you to understand that old habits die hard. New people who are not expected to be somewhere have always put us on edge. Intellectually, we know that there is no way you are part of a grand scheme, but emotionally, we are still afraid."

"Well, there is no more CIA or FBI for you to check with." Sofie is not as stoic as Ms. Crenshaw. "I thought that all of us survivors would pull together to get through this. If that's not the case, someone should let me know now."

"Sofie. We're with you 100 percent." Grace is physically and emotionally behind her friend.

"Paddrick made it quite clear last night that the Robinson family is a package deal that includes you and Remmie." Jane does not seem to understand how to deal with other emotional people. "He explained the circumstances of your meeting and I have no reason to believe you are anything other than friendly."

"Well someday maybe I can say the same about you." Sofie gets up and leaves the room quickly. Grace follows after her immediately.

"Donna?" Dad is looking at Mom and waiting for her to speak. They did not sort things out last night. Her only response is to sit carefully in the chair beside her.

"I'm sorry if anyone is uncomfortable." Jane is moving on to another agenda item. "I understand that your journey from

New Hampshire was unpleasant. It is completely within reason to think that you need a day or two to adjust and settle in. Cassandra and I have been finding solace in continuing our work at Ames and we intend to maintain that practice."

"Hold on." I am not being polite. "You work for the government and have admitted to talking with the CIA and the FBI. Is there anything we should know about this virus that seems to have killed the rest of the world?"

"NASA, young man, is hardly the government." She is condescending and slightly offended. "I spoke with the FBI and the CIA in my capacity as a parent and United States citizen, not as an employee of the space agency. To insinuate that I have more details about this horrible epidemic is insulting."

"Is there anyone else that you would not be surprised to see?" Dad is taking this down a more pertinent route.

"Do you mean to ask if I am aware of other survivors?" A flash of emotion in her face hints at the answer, and we all notice her look towards Mom. "The answer is yes. There are others who seem to have survived."

"And are the other survivors also government employees?" Dad intentionally ties her back to the government.

"They do work in facilities with ties to the Unites States government but I am not sure who provided funding for their paychecks." Jane gives an honest but not enlightening answer.

"Are you in contact with them? Are they coming here?" Dad is losing patience.

"We are in contact with them and, while they would like to join us, they are not currently in transit." She is not offering anything that was not asked.

"You know this would go a lot smoother and I would be a lot more comfortable if you didn't make us play fifty questions." Dad is done messing around. "In fact, I know what will make it go even smoother. Us leaving. Thanks for the room and board, good luck surviving in your bubble."

"Wait," Jane rises from the table in an overly controlled

manner. "I would like it if you stayed."

"Don't make me ask another question then." Dad is not playing games.

"There is a global community of scientists that have been receiving a 'super vaccination' for years." Jane has walked over to stand behind Cassandra. "The vaccination was intended to protect against a wide range of potential pandemics. It was felt that if a large portion of the Earth's population were destroyed, the scientific community would be best suited for rebuilding."

"Then how do you explain the seven of us?" I don't feel like she's being honest.

"After Seamus finished eighth grade, the government approached me about having him participate in the vaccine program. I was able to negotiate the whole family into the program." Mom is studying the wood of the tabletop.

"Then how do you explain Remmie and Sofie?" I ask, focusing on Jane.

"I don't." Jane looks around the room at each of us, seeming to linger on Mom. "Perhaps you have good genes? Sadly not all those vaccinated fared as well as Cassandra and me. Many of them are dead. Those who survived are staying connected with us through a secure and highly redundant version of the Internet. It includes radio towers and solar-powered relay stations. Even in the event that power is lost at the national level, we will be able to remain in contact."

"I can tell you that power *is* lost at the national level. It is a reality, not an eventuality." Dad has no interest in helping her maintain a warped perception of our situation.

"Well that explains some of the delays in communications." Jane is processing something. "Perhaps we can discuss this further over dinner? Cassandra and I really should be getting down to Ames. There are simulations and experiments that need to be tended to and analyzed. Seamus, I think you should join us. You will no doubt find our work fascinating."

"I agree, Seamus, I think you should go with them. I've told them so much about your lab and your passion for physics. They would be happy to show you around." Mom has not physically moved but she is on "their" side.

The lights flicker, reminding us that we need to move forward, not sit idly.

"I don't think you three understand the situation we are in here." Dad is flabbergasted. "There is no FBI, CIA or even NASA anymore. In fact, I would probably say that there is no East coast anymore. Everything from Chicago to Boston has been burned in the wildfire we survived. You don't need to wait for orders from someone else. If you are not working to secure food, water and shelter for yourself, you are going to die."

"Well you can choose to live with that approach." Jane is heading to the door. "I choose to live with the approach of 'Keep Calm and Carry On.' I have faith that our country will rebound from this disaster."

"Seamus, would it really hurt to see what they are working on for a day?" Mom is nearly pleading with me. "I'll show everyone else around the Bay area. Dad can make lists and worry about the things that concern him, and tonight, if there are still questions, we can continue to talk openly."

I want to shake her and yell, "Mom, wake up, it's me Seamus!" But I can't move. Then it dawns on me; maybe she has a plan. Maybe she wants me to go along with things and figure out what they are up to. I'm not a good actor, so she won't let me in on the plan, but she needs me involved because of something advanced they are working on.

"How about we head down to this Ames place and you guys come meet us for lunch?" I want to be involved but I'm scared about spending the day alone with these two. "That way they'll have some time to show me around without being interrupted and maybe I'll find some place to set up my lab."

"That would allow all of you to get a vaccine booster, too." Cassandra has not lost the fact that there are some of us who are still "at risk."

"How often do we need to get these vaccine boosters?" I had almost forgotten about them.

"Boosters are given quarterly," Jane says, as if there are no options to stray from the schedule, even though we are totally off schedule already. Then, without further words, she rises from her chair and leaves the room.

Dad looks at me and I can't tell if he understands that I want to trust Mom on this. We have been communicating so well lately that I don't want this to cause a breakdown between us.

"Whatever you want to do." He is shaking his head. "We'll see you in a few hours," he says, and leaves the room.

CHAPTER 24

I am in the backseat of a silver E-Class Mercedes. We're crawling along at 65 miles an hour and I wonder what I've gotten myself into. Dad always used to say that a black Mercedes S 500 whispered elegance. It's a true luxury car without the *hey look at me* nature of a Bentley or a Rolls Royce. He also liked the sportiness available in the C-Class Mercedes, but he was not a fan of the E-Class. "A vehicle for pretenders," he calls it.

These two pretenders might be robots. They sit in their front seats staring straight ahead. Classical music is on the radio but at a maddeningly low volume. I know it's there, I can hear it, but not well enough to make out what it is. If this didn't seem so routine for them and so in-line with the personalities I've seen, I would think they are messing with me. I suppose they could be messengers bringing me to me Ames where scientists will poke, prod and dissect me to figure out why I didn't die from the "killer cold." But no, they wouldn't have waited for me. They would have taken Mom already.

I might as well try and liven things up.

"So what are you two ladies working on?" I'm light and bubbly in a way that is not characteristic.

"We're studying the energy transfer from light particles as

they collide with a variety of newly formed materials." Cassandra has her answer well-rehearsed. I'm not sure if this is a benefit or a curse of working in a university setting.

The first thing that comes to my mind is the paper on the solar sail that I read back home before the pandemic wiped out the planet. Much like a regular sail transfers the energy from the wind as it collides with the cloth, there will need to be a substance to allow the transfer of energy from light. While I did not see the Crenshaw name in the paper, I suspect that this is what they are working on. My new self sees value in the deception of having your research published by another. This unrelated person happily takes credit for your work. If it is disproved, they also take the fall—not only on this topic, but their credibility as a whole. If they are not disproved, you can capitalize on your head start by implementing the technology while others are trying to disprove it.

"Cool, like for a new kind of solar panel?" I'm going to play dumb. They are keeping things from me; I need to keep some things from them.

They both fall for my act. They exchange a glance with smiles and the slightest of head shakes indicating to each other that I must not "get it." It may turn out to be easier to manipulate these two than I had thought. I guess that manipulating smart people, whether their intelligence is real or perceived, is easier than manipulating people of average intelligence. They think that they are so smart that no one will out-think them. People of average intelligence are wary of being duped and keep their minds on reality, not the perception.

"Not really. It's some pretty advanced stuff." Jane is back to focusing on the road, seemingly very proud of herself. "But your mom did mention that you had been working on some kind of power pack. Are you interested in solar power?"

Now she is trying to manipulate me. I'm not used to these mind games; do I let her think she's manipulating me so that I can continue to manipulate her? Or do I call her out now and tell her she shouldn't be so obvious?

"Not really solar, but definitely using energy particles to generate electricity." My answer is honest and kind of vague. I'm going to keep up with the charade.

"Did you ever make any progress on your idea or is it still something you have up on the drawing board?" Cassandra is friendlier than her mother.

"I was pretty close before all this happened." Also true, but much harder to play games when I think about all the people who have died. "Speaking of which, what are you going to do for power when the grid goes down?"

"We have a backup diesel generator. It will run the lab at full capacity for 24 hours." Jane is confident that she has all the answers. "If we operate in the most basic communications-only mode, we can run for 48 hours."

"So two days after the grid goes down, you'll decide to start worrying about survival?" I can't believe that they don't get it. "Or do you know how to drive a tractor-trailer truck and feel comfortable refueling the diesel generator every day?"

There are no answers to my questions. I don't know if I have spurred a thought in them that makes the future problems more obvious. Maybe not talking anymore helps them enjoy their denial for a time longer. I'm okay with the silence, but it doesn't bode well for the psyche of these two learned women.

Ames is beautiful. I can see the famous Hangar 1, impossible to miss at 200 feet tall and more than 1,000 feet long. The sign reads "Ames Research Center" on top and "NASA Research Park" underneath. The gate is closed and there are no obvious signs of other people. Perhaps I was sitting in silence to protect my own psyche and not address my fears of encountering human's intent on harming my family or me.

I now find it funny that I never had aspirations to work in a facility like this. In fact, I never really thought about the future beyond completing my power reactor. In hindsight, I think that I assumed I would make money from selling the reactor or licensing its design. I know Mom could have helped us get rich marketing the technology. Then I suppose I would have built my own lab in a warehouse in Nashua or another southern New Hampshire town and lived and worked around where I grew up. The money would have been nice, but I was never interested in fame.

Jane has parked the car in a space labeled "Crenshaw." There was no hesitation or even thought of finding another space, even though there are almost no cars in the lot. I want to ask her why she didn't just drive up to the door of whichever building she works in, but I hold my tongue. Something has to rock her world soon. I don't think it will come from me.

They both exit the car with purses and laptop bags in hand. Without a word to me, they head off toward a brick nondescript building. Part of me wants to just sit in the car and see what they do. The other part of me wants to get out and explore. This is an advanced research campus. I had become desensitized to the halls of MIT and Harvard, but this is new. There is a new library to find hidden treasures in, labs with different approaches to discovery. There is so much I could do here.

I climb out of the car but do not follow the Crenshaws. It's a power move to just leave me here alone. They must know that I am dying to get in a lab and start playing. I need to calm down and get control. They want me excited; they want to use potential to control me. Deep breath time. Remember, it's me versus them. It's okay to follow along as long as I look for openings on the way.

I jog to catch up with them, but I am too far back for them to even hold the door. It seems like their pace has slowed, but that may be because I want it to. I see them go up the stairs and through the doors at the top. Bounding up two steps at a time, I am just able to see them turn into a doorway. I do my best to regain a little composure and walk through the doors at the top of the stairs. Instead of pausing at the doorway, I walk right in, finding myself in a conference room.

"Sparring with you on the ride was fun." Jane is leaning on

the conference table with both hands, and her tone is menacing. "However, I did not become the Senior Director for Intergalactic Engagement by sparring with 16-year-old hacks. Sit down, Mr. Robinson."

I'm nervous that once I sit down orderlies will come into the room and secure me to the chair. Once they have me restrained there will be no sense in fighting. I have almost no tolerance for pain and my lack of athleticism is clear. But she is an adult and she is scolding me; somewhere in my head, years of school and classroom experience have me sliding into the closest chair.

"Cassandra and I reviewed your reactor plans four years ago." Jane might as well be rubbing her hands together like an evil doctor. "The FBI detected a pattern in your Google research that had them worried you were trying to build some type of bomb. During their research, they found enough of your chat room transcripts to guess that you were working on an advanced reactor. They asked us to take a look at your efforts to help them identify if you were just a crackpot or if you were using the reactor as a cover story for something more deadly."

If they want me off-guard, they've got it. But four years ago is an eternity. My work has come so far since then.

"Let me guess. You beat me to my own invention?" I can't see the point of this performance.

"No. We determined that you were just a crackpot." Cassandra can't let her mother have all the fun.

"So it's a coincidence that you know me, met my mother after the apocalypse and now have me here in your secret lair?" The point of all this is lost on me.

"Not coincidence, but unlikely possibility. My only guess is that there were others who saw some merit in your work. They must have believed that either your thought process or your invention were significant enough to include you in the vaccination program." Jane continues to look like she has an evil plan she's about to reveal.

"Well, I'm not sure what your point is." Now I think she

may be bluffing all of her bravado. "Are you upset that there were significantly smarter people out there who understood my work or are you hoping that I'll teach you what I know?"

"Hah!" It's a statement more than a laugh. "Son, I think you jumped on the anti-super symmetry bandwagon a little too soon. Cassandra and I are a matter of weeks away from what we think will prove super symmetry once and for all. Just because it's not as elegant as we had hoped does not mean it's not accurate."

"Interesting point." I have them on the ropes and they don't even know it. "I had proven super symmetry wrong before I even knew the theory existed. Not only that, but I am days away from building a power reactor that proves I'm correct. I don't *think* I'm right. I know it."

"I've seen smarter people than you fail," Jane interrupts.

"Hold on, it gets better," I say. "Pretty soon, you are going to lose power. Unless you let me build my reactor to supply your lab with electricity, you won't be able to complete your work to see that you were wrong. So really I'll get to see you proven wrong twice." Smug works very well for me.

"I think your doom and gloom are misguided." Jane has been knocked down a peg but she is not giving in. "We have our own power plant and generators. We are not going to lose power."

As if on cue, the lights in the conference room go out. I wish I had been near a light switch so that I could have done it just to mess with her, but this is better.

"Well, good luck getting your power plant back online. Or maybe troubleshooting that generator you have been touting will be easier." I rise from my seat. "I'm going outside to wait for my family. Once they arrive, we'll get out of your hair forever."

I walk out the door full of self-confidence. I'm the James Bond of nerds. I just went head-to-head with not one but two NASA physicists and won. I go down the stairs two at a time, the same way I went up. I push through the door and out into daylight. Even this late in the fall, the California sun is warm and comforting. I walk casually across the parking lot towards the gate; I plan to wait on the other side.

"Seamus, wait!" Cassandra hurries through the door. "You know how suspicious it seems that our two families met up? What does it matter? My mother and I didn't get to make the decision on who was in the program and who was not. We certainly didn't cause this virus to be released. I'm sorry we don't know the right way to act."

"Well, I never spied on you and your mother." I am only stopping long enough to fully close the door on this experience.

"We never really spied on you. I was handed some data and asked to evaluate it. I was never told that there would be consequences to my analysis." She is shaking her head. Maybe she is tired of the lies and deception, too. "We're a little old for this, but I'll show you mine if you show me yours?" Cassandra is looking kind of coy. "Scientifically speaking, of course."

"Facts only, no opinion?" I would like to see what they have.

"Facts only." She holds out her hand to shake on it.

CHAPTER 25

The three hours in front of the white board have been a battle. In addition to me being rusty from a few days away from hard-core physics, I'm sure that the two concussions I received are not helping. Additionally, I am not a formally trained physicist; I've generally taught myself. Some of the language and approaches Cassandra uses take time to adjust to, but I am quick to adapt.

Even though it has not been easy, it's fun. It's like finally being able to talk with another fan about our favorite team. There is not a lot of arguing, per se, but we stop to remind each other of facts that we consider obscure or potentially in doubt. Cassandra is very intelligent and well-spoken. I'm a little surprised that Jane has let Cassandra run the discussion, but as I watch her face, I think she may be struggling to keep up.

I'm pretty sure we are nearing the end of her presentation and there are only one or two areas that I would like to debate. They have done solid work, but inherently I know it is flawed. I can see how these particles go together, and my tests have proven me to be correct. There must be one big assumption they are making that I can grab onto and show them it is wrong.

The honk of a car horn startles me more than just a little.

The Crenshaw's seem unfazed. I wonder if they even consider the possibility of paramilitary groups or other bad people being alive? Apart from the roadblock, I have no reason to fear other people, but it's still in my mind that we are not alone. Even a hint of caution from Jane or Cassandra would make me feel just a little bit better. Instead they remain emotionless and show no physical reaction.

"I believe that is your family arriving," Jane says with a quick glance to her watch. "Would you like to take a break and go retrieve them?"

We don't need to spend any more time on their flawed theory. I am going to show them the basis for my power reactor. I've never shared this with another person before. My thinking is that if I don't have it implemented in the real world, I shouldn't write it down as fact. But the truth is I will have it implemented in a matter of days; of this I am certain. Cassandra and Jane will always remember where they were the first time they saw this formula.

"I'll go get them in a second," I say as I walk to the whiteboard and grab a marker. "While I'm outside, though, I would like you to spend some time thinking about this." I'm writing on the board quickly but in full control. The long and highly complex equation is completed fast and without mistakes. Before stepping back and moving my body to reveal the whole thing, I look at it in awe. It is beautiful; I am a genius.

After my self-congratulations, I walk towards the door to leave. I feel good knowing I am the smartest person in the room. In a physics throw-down, I just schooled them.

"But wait." Cassandra is stopping me. "We said no opinions."

"That's all fact." I'm focusing on her, not even looking at the board.

"Well then, it's not reality." Her smirk makes it clear that she thinks she has me. "There is no point in sending the amount of energy needed to generate this reaction to infinity."

"What if it results in a bell curve?" is all I have to say to send them scrambling. "Why don't you run through this for a while. I'm going downstairs to let my family through the gate and we are going to walk around a little bit."

Like so many other geniuses and "experts," Cassandra and Jane have been blinded by science. They have taken long-standing limitations and assumptions as fact. They are so smart they were never naive enough to ask what would happen if they questioned a long-held limitation. As a child inventor, I always considered the power coming out of the wall as limitless. When I started putting my ideas into mathematical equations, I always had the energy used to start a reaction move to infinity. After countless experiments and swapping of variables, I found the one element that would create a bell curve for the release of energy. You get more power out then you put in. In fact, as the energy input trends to zero, the energy output trends to infinity. So once you get the reaction started, it is easy to not only power itself, but to take excess power out.

Outside, it's no surprise that Dad found a way through the gate. He has parked the Escalade next to Jane's Mercedes. He had no idea what building we were in, so he couldn't get the car any closer to us. When they see me, there is no mad dash to meet up. It's only been a few hours, but I'm worried that they think I have been brainwashed.

"How was your morning?" Dad is looking at me for signs of something being off.

"We went in the Pacific Ocean!" Liam can't contain his excitement and starts talking before Dad is even finished.

"Cool. It's cold up here in Northern California, isn't it?" I know I have to get Liam taken care of before I can really talk with Dad.

"A little bit. But it was still kind of awesome." Liam is smiling and sees something off in the distance that he wants to explore.

"Everything okay?" Dad again.

"Fine, I guess." I'm not sure how to explain the morning we had. "The drive down got a little weird. We eventually switched to nerd mode though, and have been talking physics for a few hours."

"Is there anyone else here?" Dad is not relaxed.

"I haven't seen or heard anything suspicious. The truth is, though, we went straight into a conference room and haven't really come out." Now I'm a little edgy, thinking about commandos.

"I'm going to poke around a little bit." Dad turns to survey the gate and parking lot entrance.

"I wish you would stop it with this S.W.A.T. thing you are trying to do. You have been on edge all morning." Mom is clearly continuing a conversation that she and Dad have been having. "If anyone wanted to capture you, they would have done it by now."

"Stop being so simple-minded." Dad is not having a conversation, he's ending one. "The major from the roadblock said he had sent survivors to rally in San Francisco. Sofie and Remmie are proof that people who were not vaccinated could have survived. Do you want to throw away your efforts to get us in the program by not protecting ourselves?" He heads off to the first building in the circle. For some reason, I won't feel safe until he does.

"Mom, why are you and the Crenshaws so confident that we are totally safe?" I can't help but engage her on how she has such a different perspective than the rest of her family.

"I wouldn't lump me and the Crenshaws in the same pile." Mom is smiling a little. "Jane and Cassandra seem to expect a bus or airplane to arrive any minute full of people who are going to take care of everything. It's as if they believe a score of government employees are hiding out in bunkers around the country, waiting for some signal it's safe to come out. They may be right, but I doubt it."

"Well, what do you think then?" She hasn't covered her point of view yet.

"Me?" She looks at the ground. "I'm with your father that most everyone is dead. I differ in the fact that I'm not afraid of survivors. If we find someone alive, they are going to be scared and hungry, like Sofie and Remmie. There are no black jumpsuits that want to dissect our brains."

She was a little dramatic with the "dissect our brains" comment, but I agree that this is Dad's fear. A fear I share. We have proof that people could survive the virus, and Jane thinks I may have been secretly vaccinated against it. Anyone with half an ounce of delusional power would see this as an opportunity. I can't speak for Dad, but from my perspective, even if someone *didn't* engineer this, the opportunity could create a villain.

"Maybe if you'll agree to be a little more cautious, we can agree to be a little less..." I can't think of the word to finish my thought.

"Militant?" Mom finishes for me.

"Fair enough." I don't like the word but it probably fits. "I'll talk to Dad about toning it down with the guns if you'll agree that we should at least keep them nearby?"

"That will probably make us all more comfortable." Mom is smiling at me. "Thank you for bailing us out as usual, Seamus."

"Have you spent time here with the Crenshaws?" I want to know what Mom knows about this facility.

"Honestly, Seamus?" She thinks I am continuing our discussion about being afraid of people.

"I'm just looking for a place to set up my lab." My face shows my innocence. "So far, all I have seen is one conference room. I thought that if you had spent time here exploring you might know of a good place for me to work."

"Oh." She looks sheepish. "I thought—well, never mind what I thought. I have not spent any time here. They told me it was pretty isolated and boring. I have been staying back at their house, sitting by the fire and reading good books."

"So instead of looking for people, maybe you can help me look for lab space?" I'm walking towards the Escalade. "I want to check on my equipment so I can also see if there are any components that need replacing."

I step up on the tire and pull myself up to the roof rack. It only takes me a second to pop the closures on the carriers and flip the top off. Inside is a shambles. Not only does it look like every motherboard and hard drive has been broken into a 100 pieces, any plastic has been melted. My lab is ruined. I don't know what the impact will be on developing my reactor. I always said the technology was just tools and the invention was all me.

It's not the end of the world. I need to act, or more importantly, react, like an adult. An adult who has just lost almost ten years of creativity, sweat and sacrifice. Everyone else may see this stuff as just computer parts or garbage, but it was my whole world. "Disappointment" doesn't seem like a strong enough word. On the other hand, "devastation" seems overly dramatic.

"What's the story?" Dad is back from surveying the perimeter. "Need a hand unpacking your gear?"

"Nope," I'm going to try for upbeat. "It's all junk. Looks like whatever didn't melt in the fire got trashed in the crash."

"Oh Seamus, I'm so sorry." Mom comes to my side and puts an arm around my shoulders. "I know that lab represented years of scavenging and hacking. You worked so hard on each and every component."

"I guess I have to try and think about the good news." I look at both of them. "My code was all backed up on the network and there is nothing in these carriers I can't replace with a little hard work. Instead of putting together another hack-lab, I get to build an awesome new lab."

"A positive attitude is going to come in handy a lot in the coming months." Dad has his hand on my shoulder. I guess this gesture has replaced the hug now that I'm an adult. "It's okay to be disappointed, but moving forward is key. Do you want me to find a Dumpster for this stuff?"

"Paddrick! Give him at least a minute to be sad." Mom slaps him on the shoulder.

"Yeah, why don't you just throw the carrier and everything right in. That stuff is from the old world. I want to build something for the new world." Now I see opportunity in front of me.

CHAPTER 26

I could live in a bubble, too, if things kept going my way. Power came back on while Dad and I threw the rooftop carriers in the Dumpster. It's funny that I have a physical sensation of feeling lighter now that the lab is gone. My guess is that tomorrow I'll feel overwhelmed when I start the rebuilding process, but for now, I'm free.

We're driving back to San Francisco. I've agreed to ride with Jane and Cassandra so we can continue our discussion on my reactor. The two of them have handled things remarkably well. We spent the afternoon in the conference room going between the whiteboard and the computer display we've projected on the wall. They have moved from doubt to suspicion, and I almost have them to acceptance.

"I still don't understand how you came up with the idea for your containment field." Jane stopped questioning the physics about thirty minutes ago. Now she seems to be focused on the process.

"I'm not sure how to answer that." The truth is the idea just sort of came to me. "I was thinking about how magnets and copper wire generate electricity with no waste. The waste comes from whatever is used to make the magnets move around the wire. Then the idea just came to me."

"How do you know it will be stable?" Cassandra is more focused on the hard science. "I can envision a number of scenarios that don't end well."

"In addition to common sense?" My question is rhetorical. "We live in a balanced system. That was the super-symmetry point you were trying to make this morning. I'm not moving anything to the other side of the seesaw, just rearranging the things on our side."

We go on like this for the entire ride, Jane looking for sources behind my knowledge and Cassandra looking for proof of components I consider fact. I get the impression that they would both prefer to be doing this in a lecture hall under more formal circumstances. While I am a big fan of structure and documentation, it is an odd experience.

We pull up to the garage door at the Crenshaw home and Jane instinctively presses the button on the garage door remote. It has no effect. Naturally, she presses it again. The door does not open. It wasn't user error that prevented the door from going up. The light beside the back door is not on and there is no glow from inside the building. San Francisco has lost power.

"Looks like the power is out." I can't resist.

"Well I'm sure that it will be back soon." Jane can't help but count on her luck.

We get out of the car and Jane unlocks the back door. As we shuffle in, I have a feeling that the Crenshaw bubble is about to burst. Electricity doesn't need a coffee break. It didn't pause to catch its breath before going back to work. Something broke, and there is no lineman heading out to repair it.

At home we have a gas stove. Even when the electricity goes out in a blizzard, we can cook on the stove. The Crenshaws have an electric cooktop and no gas appliances. There will be no gourmet dinner tonight.

Jane and Cassandra try their best to go about what must be a regular routine. The car keys are hung up and purses are placed on a chair. I believe that at some point there was a magazine or newspaper involved in their evening ritual. That was either replaced by a tablet long ago or eliminated when delivery stopped a few weeks ago.

Cassandra opens the refrigerator and squints at the contents inside. With no light in the fridge or in the kitchen, taking inventory is difficult. Clearly she is not experienced in loss-of-power situations. She should keep the door to the fridge closed and not flush the toilets.

"Maybe you could go round up some candles." Dad puts his hand on the refrigerator door and pushes it closed. "We'll take care of dinner tonight."

I would have expected more of a protest from them. Instead, both Jane and Cassandra head off to another part of the house. I'm sure that they have a perfect assortment of candles in a very specific location. It's not like they need to find them; they need to get them.

When we finally sit down to eat, Dad does not have food in front of him. My first thought is one of concern that he is ill and will be coughing soon. The dining room is quiet and awkward. Five of us have become accustomed to scavenging for dinner and eating in less-than-traditional settings. There are three adults that are learning to accept inconvenience and eating for sustenance, not pleasure or comfort.

"I tested all the ingredients before I served them. Everything on the table is safe, and I'm a little full." Dad is smiling. "We need to talk about tomorrow and the rest of our future."

There are no objections.

"We should permanently relocate to Ames." He specifically watches Jane for her reaction, but there is none. "Not only is it self-contained with its own power substation and backup generators, it has a reasonable security perimeter. I know that you have been comfortable here since things happened, but I don't expect power to return. I'm sure the commute seems better with no cars on the road, but we need to think about conserving every resource we have. Not just gas and food, but time and energy, too."

"Could we have some time in the morning to pack up a

few things?" Cassandra is speaking for both of them. "There are some housing units we can move into down there. We'll be able to move around on foot or by bicycle if we restrict our world to the campus."

They must have foreseen this day coming. It can't be that big of a surprise, but they are reacting as if they just realized that the population of the planet has been erased. I suppose that the shock of realizing something that you have known for a time is more stressful than instant recognition.

"After we eat, I'll go out and retrieve a box truck or something to help move your personal effects. I'll also gather some breakfast food so we can all eat before we try and do anything strenuous." Dad is careful with his tone and trying to keep an even temper.

Dinner didn't really end; it sort of just stopped happening. Mom excused herself and did not come back. Then Grace and Sofie announced that they were going to take Remmie up to bed. I waited around thinking that we could talk more about my reactor, but Jane and Cassandra were not in a chatty mood. Liam went out with Dad to help locate a moving truck and breakfast foods. I was left to finally go up to my room alone and let myself fade off to sleep thinking about how to build a new and better lab.

Today is another early morning for me. I'm a little lost, not having to worry about what is going to happen or where we are going to spend the night. Once we get to Ames, it will be our home for good. No temporary lodging or reason for keeping our things packed away. I never moved as a kid, but it seems like settling into a new home is easy. Rebuilding my lab will be work.

We all help move the suitcases and a few select pieces of furniture. Dad has to veto a few items that are too hard to move, but in general he is pretty generous with what he puts effort into for them. Jane and Cassandra share some memories while we work, but they do not seem original or deep. I suddenly feel like this home was for show and that they used it as a tool to progress their careers or their perceived standing in the community. My gut tells me that they have real memories down at Ames and will actually be more comfortable once we all live there.

Dad and Liam drive the box truck while Sofie drives Mom, Grace and Remmie down in the Escalade. Somehow I wind up riding with Jane and Cassandra. The trip is quiet and I spend my time thinking about what I should be thinking about. Yesterday we were guests in their pre-apocalyptic world. Today they are permanent residents in our post-apocalyptic nightmare. We have the upper hand of experience, but they have home field advantage. It seems the playing field is level. I hope we can work together as a team.

We pull into the parking lot at Ames and everyone gets out of the vehicles. There is an awkward moment of silence, but Jane surprises me as the first one to speak.

"I know that Ames is 'our; space, but I want you all to do what you need to make parts of it your own. We would both appreciate the privilege of keeping our lab building and the museum intact, but other than that, I can't see much reason to treat these spaces with reverence."

"Seamus, I know that you are hoping to rebuild your lab, but Mother and I would like to invite you to join us in working in our space." Cassandra is looking at me directly. "Before we begin unloading, I will show you where the component supply warehouse is located, so that you can get anything you need to progress with your reactor development."

"Thank you." I'm not sure if I should speak before Mom or Dad says something, but why not. "I have a lot to think about before rebuilding my lab and it doesn't seem like there is much need to rush. I can help unload and work on making this place feel more like home."

"We respectfully disagree." Cassandra is still speaking for both she and her mother. "If all your calculations are truly correct, you will need a huge power surge to initiate your device. Even our massive generators will not be able to generate that level of surge. You need to get your reactor built and get it working before our plant fails."

I thought that using the generators to initiate the reaction might be a problem. I haven't run through the calculations yet, so I don't like to say that it will be impossible. That being said, I need to take this opportunity to prove myself.

"Well, I hope that version of the redundant secure network you mentioned the other night can get me to my cloud." I'm ready to drop everything to focus on my reactor.

"I think you will be pleasantly surprised with what we are able to connect you with." Cassandra is feeling pretty self-confident herself.

"Fine. Why don't you nerds get to work on your computer stuff." Dad is not interested in joining our little love fest. "The rest of us are going to explore the campus. While we are living together as a community, I think we should have a central food storage and dining facility. We cannot afford to waste food or water."

"Paddrick, before you head off to explore, I would like to speak with you for a minute." Jane is walking closer to Dad and it seems like she wants to speak with him in private. "I have a rather large request I would like you to consider."

Cassandra is walking off towards the building we spent time in yesterday. She didn't wait to be dismissed or ask for permission. I fall in behind her and work on shifting my mind over to the reactor. My first priority has to be downloading code and the right build environment from my cloud storage. Second will be to get the components together to begin the manufacturing process.

"Let's start in the supply room." Cassandra is talking over her shoulder as she walks. We are in the hallway of the building, about to pass the stairs up to the conference room we were in yesterday.

"I'd rather go to the lab and begin downloading some things that might take a while." I am skilled at multi-tasking when it comes to waiting for bits and bytes to travel across the network.

"Well, you should have a new workstation for that." She opens the door and flips a light switch.

The room is filled with workstations and monitors. The walls are lined with bins of processors, circuit boards and memory blocks. It is a geek candy store. The supply is not unlimited, but it is more than I will need to build not only a killer lab, but *several* reactors, if need be. I can see that everything is labeled and there appear to be spec sheets hanging from each bin. There will be no need to guess what a component is good at before testing it out. This will be the first real development environment I have ever worked in. The efficiencies will be abundant. I can't wait to get started.

"Why don't you poke around for a bit?" Cassandra can tell that I am excited and trying to decide what to check out first. "I'm going to grab a cart so we can bring things upstairs without having to carry them."

CHAPTER 27

Working with Cassandra is not easy. She is smart. Not quite my level, but smart enough to ask questions about everything I need her to do. There have been a few areas where her questions resulted in modifications that will improve my reactor. However, in general, I ask her to do something, we argue about it, she does it, and finds out that I was right.

Part of me is jealous when she thinks of something that will improve my idea. I keep reminding myself that I have invented the most advanced piece of technology in the history of mankind. There would be no tweaks or enhancements if I hadn't come up with the idea in the first place. Cassandra must think that she is something special to be making improvements on something this advanced.

While there is a physical attraction to her, I don't like her.

That's not actually true. It's more like I don't think anything of her. She's there. I don't hate her, but if she were gone, I wouldn't be upset. It's kind of sad to think that, because there are not many other people left in the world. Both of the Crenshaws are kind of stiff and robotic. It's always "mother," never "mom" or, god forbid, "ma." In the other direction, it's always "Cassandra," never "Cassie" or "sweetheart." I don't think my Dad would have ever spoken to me if he couldn't use a nickname or pet name. Maybe they have developed this approach as a way to remain professional at work? At any rate, the lab feels icy and detached.

I have been working for almost 20 hours straight. It feels good to be back at this full tilt. My new self-awareness has me recognizing that my execution is slipping as I get more tired. Interestingly though, my creativity seems to be on the rise the more tired I get. I would like to get the containment fields complete before I go off to sleep. I wonder if I should try and do what Einstein did and sleep for 20 minutes every 4 hours?

Just as I finish the final touches on the containment field generator, Cassandra and Jane walk into the lab. I was debating a test of the finished work, but with them here I will put it off until I can sleep a little and double-check my work.

"Good morning," I greet them pleasantly.

"Have you been in here all night?" Jane is not happy to see me.

"I guess so." I'm not sure why it matters to her. "I was kind of rolling, so I decided to keep at it. I just finished building the containment field generator."

"Please don't touch anything else." Jane is shaking her head as if I just ruined her favorite toy. "Go to bed. It may have been 'cool' back home, but here at Ames we do not do all- nighters. They are not safe and they are not efficient."

"I'm not saying it's cool." I am defensive and a little surprised that she is not impressed with me. "I've just always worked this way. The price of having to get through high school while conducting advanced research and development."

"Well there is no more high school to get in your way." She is moving on to her own things. "From now on, the lab is accessible from seven to seven and that will be it."

"I don't think I can work like that." I feel like I am arguing with my mom about bedtime. "Besides, I thought you agreed that my reactor was pretty important."

"You are working on a device that will generate gigawatts of power in a very small space." Jane is staring me down. "There is the very real possibility that a mistake could be explosive. I will not lose a life or my lab because you didn't get enough sleep."

I generally know she has a good point, but I don't like it. I'm safe. I knew not to test the containment field while I was this tired. I also know exactly how wrong things can go with this invention. There is at least one hole in the ground back home that can attest to how much power can be discharged.

"Can we make a compromise and say no more than twelve straight hours in the lab?" I want to work with her and I think this is a good idea.

"No." She does not agree with me or feel the need to elaborate.

"Well thanks for at least discussing it with me." My sarcasm is thick and not meant to be hidden.

"Seamus, there is nothing to discuss." She is getting exasperated. "I do not trust that you would limit yourself to working twelve hours. I can imagine you leaving moments before I arrived only to return, denying that you had been here. What you and Cassandra are working on is important, but safety is more important to me. I will unlock the door at seven a.m. and lock it at seven p.m. This conversation is over."

"Fine. I'll see you this afternoon." I turn on my heel and I'm out the door. I was too tired to debate effectively. Now I'm too tired to even be that mad at her.

Outside in the parking lot, the sun sends me reeling. It is a bright beautiful day and the sun saps the last ounces of drive I have in my body. I still haven't settled on a room for myself, but I know where there is a comfortable couch where I can get some sleep.

"Good morning, Seamus," Dad says to me, seemingly from out of nowhere.

"Oh hey, Dad." I'm ready to give into the exhaustion.

"You look like you could fall asleep on your feet." Dad is smiling like he knows something I don't. "I'm not going to make you go to school or anything, you know. You can work on your power pack during the day and sleep at night if you want to."

"Thanks." I'm not sure what I am thanking him for. "That won't be an issue anymore. From now on, Jane is only letting me in the lab from seven a.m. to seven p.m. She says it's a safety issue."

"Well, she's probably right." Dad is moving in a little closer to me. "I know you will adapt. You have grown up a lot in the last few days. I can't say that I'm glad for what we've gone through, but I am very proud of how you've handled it and grown."

"I love you, Dad." I grab him and hug him tightly.

"Love you, too, buddy." He breaks the embrace. "Now go get some sleep." He is off to parts unknown.

I head to the dorm or hotel or whatever we are calling it. I heard Liam and Grace argue about calling it home. He is ready to use the word, but she is not. *Home* has a connotation and a feeling for Grace that she needs time to develop. For Liam and even for me, *home* is a place—an easily transferable one at that.

There is a common area with a big leather couch that I slept on the night we moved in. It's not private, but I have no need to hide myself in a room somewhere. This is different for me. I almost hope that I will be disturbed after I get some sleep. I want to have people around and know that they are here. They used to annoy me, but now I need others to feel safe.

All is quiet around the house. My guess is that everyone else is still asleep. There is a small patch of sun shining on the couch. I think about how warm it will make me as I lie down and curl up under a blanket I grabbed from the top of a box in the hallway. I need to set my brain to work on connecting the reactor to the substation. If my invention is to add any value to our new society, it will need to be usable.

I wish Remmie would stop yelling. Mom likes to sleep late. Maybe she will come out and tell them to take their game outside so "normal" people can sleep. Sometimes I wonder if Mom and I are really the normal people, or if we are the ones that are different. We like to note that the way we do things is the best way to do them, but then we are both surprised that there are so few people like us. I can't believe I'm having trouble getting to sleep after that long night in the lab.

"Tag! You're it!" Remmie slaps me on the stomach and screams in my ear.

"Are you kidding me?!" I roar. Sure, I'm in a common area, but it can't be much after 7:30 in the morning.

"No, we're not kidding you." Sofie is at the foot of the couch, hands on hips. "We gave you until 4:30 in the afternoon. If you want quiet now, go find a room."

"I've been asleep all day?" I'm confused by the time.

"Yes." she is smiling now. "And I must say you are pretty cute when you're sleeping."

"Did I say anything?" Now I'm worried about dreams I don't remember. Being cute doesn't make me feel great, but it could be a lot worse.

"No. But it's not like I stood here watching you the whole time. I just looked in once or twice to see if you were still here." She has moved to sitting on the couch by my feet.

"I got in trouble for spending the night in the lab." I'm not sure why I want to tell her this. "Jane is only going to let me work between seven and seven. I think I'll be moving into a more normal schedule now, so I'll be awake during the day."

"Good. Maybe we'll see more of each other then." Her hand moves to my shin and sends a shiver of warmth through my body. "That is, after Grace and I get back."

"Back?" It's a poorly formed question, but I think she gets the idea.

"Your mom agreed to watch Remmie for us tomorrow and the next day." She is getting to her feet now. "Grace and I are going to go exploring in San Francisco. I heard there is free admission to all the museums and art galleries," she finishes, with a giggle.

"Is Liam going to go with you?" I think they need protection, but I don't want to say so.

"No." She is not confused by my question but doesn't want to talk about it. "Grace and I can take care of ourselves. Your dad is making us bring a gun and a Taser, but I know we won't need them."

"Well, enjoy the city, but please be careful." I want to ask her to stay until I can go with them.

I'm worried not only about my sister's well-being but that somehow Sofie will find that cottage by the ocean and not come back. I want to list all the dangers and perils that could be out there, but I don't want to cast a shadow on their fun. It is awkward to feel fear and worry for someone else but still to hold it in. Sharing my concerns would not be an expression of affection, but a controlling action.

Somewhere down the hall or possibly even outside, Remmie is screaming for her. "SOFIE!" can be heard in every corner of the room.

"Well guess someone needs me." She is walking towards the door. "Will I see you at dinner?"

"Definitely." I don't know what time dinner is or if I'll be done with my work, but I plan on being there.

I pull myself together and head over to the lab building. I wanted to take a shower, but between the lab closing at seven and me wanting to have dinner at the same time as Sofie, I know now is the time to get some work done.

The lab itself is quiet. I'm not sure what noises I expected to hear, but it seems there are none. It is possible that Cassandra and Jane are not even here. They may be adding a new component to their routine and stopping for tea in the late afternoon. I'm not sure where that came from but it is the first thing that popped into my head.

"Hello there," Cassandra says from behind me. "I was looking at what you put together last night and it was impressive. The only issue I have is that everything is so tight. There are a few components that will overheat if we try and operate them at capacity in such close quarters. The failure would not be dramatic, but it would be a failure no less."

"So do I need to add some cooling fins?" I hope she hasn't touched my stuff.

"No." She is not acting superior, but I can't believe she doesn't feel it. "Mother and I took the day to replicate your design on a larger scale with more appropriate clearance. I am fairly certain that your intent was to have this device remain functional for long periods of time with no maintenance. By eliminating your fascination with keeping this small, we have built something equally functional but more robust."

"Can I see it?" I'm not angry. I have never even visualized my power reactor as anything but small. It will be fascinating to see a large version of the device I see in my head.

"Sure. Liam has been helping us move the pieces over to the power substation." She grabs a tablet and a laptop. "With your help assembling the pieces tomorrow, I think we can go live in the next 48 hours."

CHAPTER 28

I'm angry, frustrated and excited. We are so close to getting my power reactor working, but I have to sit down to dinner. The containment field generators are out at the power substation. The electron gate controller is locked up tight in the lab. Jane is not going to let me in there until the morning. Maybe I should be the one who gets to drop a bomb. I don't think that Jane and Cassandra know we need a plasma converter to make the power output something we can pump into the grid.

"How are things going with the power reactor?" Dad is not asking any of us in particular.

After a long silence, Cassandra speaks. "Pretty well, I think." She looks at me to see if I want to take over. I don't. "I've learned so much from Seamus. I thought I knew about physics, but he *understands* physics. Most of my contribution is manufacturing. Even there, I couldn't work on the tiny scale that Seamus was trying to achieve."

Well she didn't have to go and be so nice about it. Now I feel like a heel for being angry with her for making a bigger version of my containment field generator.

"I personally cannot help but think about how this would have been different a month ago." Jane is narrating a story in her mind. "There would have been press coverage, offers for funding and even appearances on late night talk shows. In addition to creating an entirely new field for existing scientists to explore, there would have been countless more children inspired to pursue science."

Are they intending to make me feel bad for my attitude? Gushing doesn't suit them well. Somewhere in the back of my mind is a voice screaming "ulterior motive!"

"That's great to hear." Dad is smiling as if being my father means he's partly responsible for this accomplishment. "Beyond providing electricity to run computers, is there anything from this work that you will be able to use for pursuing your research?"

A quick glance between mother and daughter has the voice in my head screaming again.

"Hard to say." Jane has lost her talkative mood.

"When do you think that the power reactor will be ready?" Dad is not really concerned with their research.

"I think we can have it online tomorrow afternoon." Cassandra is no longer trying to defer to me.

"Probably more like a few days." I have to step in and I feel the need to knock her down a peg. "We need to come up with a plasma converter to take the reactor output and make it something we can send along the existing power lines."

"You once said it was like pumping the output from a fire hose through a garden hose." Mom wants to show she is not out of the loop.

"Right. We're going to be putting out a lot more power than we need or can handle." I like knowing the whole system.

"I have something that might work for that," Cassandra says before zoning off into deep thought mode.

Dad has a pained look on his face. We haven't really moved into talking about advanced concepts, so he can't be lost. There must be something on his mind. I'm wondering how long we have to wait for him to spit it out when he speaks.

"I didn't realize it would be ready so soon." He looks to Mom. "I was going to leave with the girls in the morning."

Why didn't Sofie tell me Dad was going with them for protection? If Dad is going, why wouldn't Mom and Liam go, too? There is something I am out of the loop on.

"I always thought you would be there the first time my reactor worked." Realizing he won't be there for that momentous first makes it seem worthless. "Where are you going?"

"I always thought I would be there for that, too." He seems to be hurt by this as much as I am. "There are a few scientists who survived in Louisiana, Texas and Arizona. I'm going to pick them up and bring them back here. I was going to have the girls drop me at a car dealership. I saw a Maserati shop not far from here." I can tell from his eyes that he will also spend the day watching over Sofie and Grace, keeping them safe.

"Oh Paddrick, I am so glad to hear that you are going for them." For the first time since we met, Jane seems genuinely pleased.

"Well, if we can count the humans left on the planet with just our fingers, it make sense to me to have us all together." He wants to make like it's not being done for her.

"As much as it excites me to think of them joining us, I believe it to be reasonable for them to wait another day." Jane likes to act like she is in control. "The scope of the accomplishment we are about to witness is not lost on me. As a mother, I also understand how you must feel about the work your son has done. I will tell them to expect your arrival no sooner than a week from tomorrow."

"Thank you." Dad has no need for conversation. "What do you say, girls? Can the San Francisco adventure wait a day or two?"

"Like you have to ask." Sofie doesn't even check with Grace before answering.

We finish dinner in a celebratory mood. I was never a part of pep rallies or tailgating before a big game, but I imagine this is what it would have felt like—getting together on the eve of a big accomplishment and celebrating the journey needed to get there.

As we filter out of the dining room, I am not tired, but instead of going for a walk or complaining about not being able to access the lab, I find a room that is not occupied. I lie down and test the bed. I lay there for a few minutes, thinking about the last few weeks. Obviously the world has changed significantly, but so have I. I am not a kid anymore. "Boy genius" is no longer fair or accurate.

I wonder if I could have completed my invention without the apocalypse occurring. It seems like there are a number of ways that would have left me one step short of completing my work. A robot servant would have been great, but it was not a necessity. Power for water and refrigeration are not nice-to-haves, they are necessities. This is why my reactor was brought to completion.

I fall asleep and start dreaming. My dream takes me to a secret government installation. They found out that I was building a power reactor and they want the technology all to themselves. There is an admiral from the Navy who says that my invention will revolutionize submarines and aircraft carriers. A colonel from the Air Force talks about planes that never need to refuel. The government has taken over my invention and is not letting me work on it when I want to.

I startle awake and realize that my current situation is not unlike my dream. Jane is a government worker. She is controlling when I can work on my reactor and what I can do with it. But I have to remember that she is not evil. There is no interest in building a weapon or using my invention for violence. Her restrictions are focused on safety, but they are restrictions nonetheless. I am going to go to the substation and start working on assembling the pieces despite the impressible hour.

At the substation, I am surprised to see Cassandra sitting quietly outside the fence. The sun is just coming up over the horizon and it is a calm morning. I don't want to startle her, but I'm afraid that calling out will do just that. I decide to shuffle my feet and walk as loudly as I can.

"Good morning, Seamus." She doesn't even look to see if it's me. "Mother will not be pleased to find out that I have been sitting here. It's not how an 'Ames researcher' would behave."

"Well sometimes we need to do things that disappoint our parents." I'm not sure what to say. I wasn't planning to come out here and talk; I'm ready to work.

"I've worked on some pretty interesting things already in my life." Cassandra looks blankly at the ground. "Never once did one of them make me want to stay up all night working."

"If all you do is sit here and stare at the ground, that will still be true tomorrow." I'm at the gate in the fence surrounding the substation. It wasn't locked; apparently Jane has no fear that I will disobey her rules. "I think we can get most of the pieces assembled and be ready for the electron gate by lunch." I have no fear of what others will think of me for wanting to work on my invention.

Without waiting for a response I am through the gate and laying out some tools before there is any motion from Cassandra. I don't care one way or the other, but in the short time we have known each other, I feel like she has earned the chance to be here. Not just be here, but to work on these final steps.

"Promise me that we will do a complete safety check *before* we initiate the reaction." She is holding onto the gate, mustering her courage to enter and disappoint her mother.

"I promise." I look at her straight in the eyes. She really is beautiful. I'm not lying either. I don't want to blow myself up or destroy what we have built. I need this to work.

"Okay." She is through the gate. "You work on that side and I'll work on this side."

We work quickly and quietly. This is what I had expected when working with a peer. Perhaps we have reached a point where Cassandra understands the reactor as well as I do. She doesn't need to ask the questions about why or how I figured it out. Even if she is not strong at coming up with new ideas, she is fantastic at running with an existing idea.

K. D. McAdams

"Good morning. It looks like you two have been at it for a while already." Jane is on the other side of the fence.

"What time is it?" I have not replaced my watch, but I may need to.

"Just after ten," Jane is calm and taking it all in visually. "I'm sure you want to get this operational today. But that will not prevent me from conducting a safety check."

"Way ahead of you on that." I don't look at her while I speak. "That's why we started a little early." It's a white lie that I hope Cassandra won't point out.

"I'll be back with some food shortly." Jane is not turning to leave. "Please be careful."

She lingered for a while in silence. I'm not sure if she was jealous, nervous or a combination of both. It is awkward to work while your boss, or at least a boss-like figure, is standing over you watching. I suppose silently is the best possible way I could have her watch; questions from her would have driven me mad.

Neither of us notices Jane leave. The sun is high in the sky and warm but comfortable. I don't think we have made a mistake or had any miscommunication in the hours we have been working. It is starting to look like the reactor I visualized in my dreams, except much larger.

Jane returns with peanut butter and jelly sandwiches, chips and sodas. She puts them down outside the gate and turns on her heel to leave. I can't figure out why she is afraid to come into the power substation.

"Mother," Cassandra startles me when she calls out. "Can I come with you? I need a bio-break and we're almost ready for the last pieces." Without addressing me she puts down her tools and heads out the gate to catch up with her mother.

When she returns, it seems like she has not even been gone long enough to get to the lab, let alone take care of other business. I've had to slow down a little bit, working both sides of the device, but my progress has been steady. I can take a bio break in the bushes nearby, and when I get back we will be ready to install the electron gate and the plasma converter.

Thinking about the plasma converter gives me pause. It is simple but elegant. Cassandra conceived of the device and built it so quickly. I better remember this next time I feel so superior to her. It is a critical element and without her it would not be available to me.

"My turn for a bio break," I say to her as we pass at the gate. I hurry over to the bushes and turn my back to the substation. I don't think she can see me, but she probably doesn't need to hear it either.

"Do you want to install the electron gate controller? I'll connect the plasma converter and complete the bridge." She's yelling so I can hear her from my crude "men's room." It's not really a question, as Cassandra is already working on the plasma converter.

"Have you ever wondered about how you could have invented a plasma converter and that happens to be exactly what is needed to connect my reactor to the grid?" I ask her, thinking to myself that it is a huge coincidence.

"Nope," is all I get in return.

The next time I look up from the reactor, I see the Escalade approaching. It parks what seems like too far away and I see Dad, Mom, Grace, Sofie, Liam and Remmie climb out. Jane is not with them. I'm not sure why they have come now, but their timing is perfect. We are so close to initiating the reaction. I can remember my dad referring to the book *The Secret* when things went well. He said that if you visualize everything working out just right, the universe would make sure that everything worked out just right.

I finish up my last bit of work and take a step back to survey the device. To me, it looks amazingly cool. As I admire my work, Cassandra steps away as well and walks over to my side. We are like two proud parents admiring our baby. I feel like I should put my arm around her and say "thank you" or "great work," but that feels like it would come across as patronizing.

"Let's take a step back before we begin the safety check." I say out loud.

We both turn and leave the fenced in area. I bend over and grab a soda and one of the sandwiches. Cassandra produces a bottle of water and grabs a bag of chips. My family is standing by quietly, ready to witness this feat of human ingenuity. Nothing could make this more perfect.

"Has anyone seen my mother?" Cassandra has identified something that could make it better, at least for her.

As if on cue, Jane's car appears on the runway and eventually comes to a stop beside the Escalade. She is elegant in the way she exits the vehicle. With no urgency or hint of intent, she walks over to us and surveys the reactor.

"Have you completed the safety check?" Her voice is icy cool.

"I was hoping you would do it," Cassandra answers. We had not discussed this, but it may be the right thing to do.

"Very well." Jane is through the gate with no ceremony and begins poring over the reactor. She is more thorough than speedy, but I expect she will be fair. There is not going to be a concern unless it is valid.

After what seems like forever, Jane exits the gate. "All appears secure. Who will be flipping the switch to initiate the reaction?"

How can that be a question? Me, of course. If there is a problem or my concept is flawed, I want to be blown up with it. I have no interest in watching my creation fall apart from a distance or to have someone die doing what I should do.

"I apologize for my poor attempt at levity." Jane is looking at me squarely. "Seamus, I am honored to be here for this historic moment. Please initiate the reaction when you are ready."

I look over at my dad. None of this would be possible without him. He gives me a big smile and thumbs up. He has his arm around Mom and they are both beaming as I walk through the gate.

Standing next to the bridge I take my signature deep breath. I can't believe that I didn't write something down to say, but now I can't wait. "Here goes," is all I get out. I flip the switch.

There is nothing but silence. After a short delay, a soft blue glow emits from the reactor. Cassandra rushes in and begins to look at the gauges and meters. I walk around and check on the plasma converter, and it is functioning as designed. Then I head over to the meters downstream from my reactor on the grid. They are all pegged at their maximum readings.

I turn to everyone watching from behind the fence. With a smile so big it hurts, I tell them, "We have power!"

The elation doesn't last long. The power will ensure that we have the vaccination for another year or so. It will help us keep food longer, have lights and computers, but it cannot reverse the annihilation of the human race. My invention is not world-changing; in fact, it barely maintains the status quo.

Before walking over to join my family, I look down at the ground. I think about all I have learned in the last few weeks. A shiver goes down my spine as I think of the possibility of surviving the virus without my family. My days of wanting to be left alone so I can pursue my work are over.

I look up and survey my Dad and Mom standing together. Grace is holding Remmie in her arms and Sofie is right next to her. Liam is ducking behind Sofie, playing hide-and-seek with Remmie. This is my future. These are the reasons I will get up every morning and try to make life better.

My signature deep breath is all that's left before walking over to join most of what's left of the human race.

AUTHOR NOTE

Thank you for reading. The Seamus Chronicles is a very personal story; the Robinson family is modeled after my own. My wife and I have a daughter adopted from China, a biological son and a son adopted from Ethiopia. My kids are still younger than the characters in the story but with the exception of the apocalypse and the genius this is how I imagine them as teenagers. Writing the character of Donna was a struggle. If I wrote her the way that I see my wife she would have been too perfect to be believable. Believable characters are always my goal, even if their situation is fiction.

I have been helped and humbled by the support, feedback and encouragement of so many people. To share your thoughts with me directly please send a note to kd@kd-mcadams.com. Engaging with readers is a true joy and influences my writing and my stories.

If you have time to write a review it is greatly appreciated. Your input will be read and taken seriously, it is the best way for me to improve my prose and plot. Reviews are important for writers and readers in that they help people to connect with the books and authors they will enjoy.

The Seamus Chronicles

Annihilation – Book 1

Evacuation – Book 2

Colonization – Book 3

Confrontation – Book 4

Connect with K. D. McAdams online:

http://kd-mcadams.com

Sign up for my newsletter to learn about new releases:

http://kd-mcadams.com/newsletter/

Twitter:

@K_McAdams

Email:

kd@kd-mcadams.com

ABOUT THE AUTHOR

K. D. McAdams writes stories about young people who make choices with their heart and not their head. 'Don't talk to strangers' is the most common phrase in our house, I have failed several art classes and I can't remember what I ate for breakfast. However I have a son that loves to talk to strangers, my daughter is an incredible artist and I have another son that is a stickler for details with a near eidetic memory. We nurture our kid's everyday with advice and information but deep down they all have an element of nature that overrides our nurturing and influences their choices. Kids who have the courage to follow their nature and make their own choices are the ones who make life memorable. When I am not writing, revising or reading a book I enjoy golfing, gardening and watching Formula 1 racing. My first book, Annihilation - Book 1 of The Seamus Chronicles is now available on Amazon.